D1563637

PLEASE PASS THE
THE
BARBIE SHOES

by

Meghan D. Lemery

Open Door Publishers, Inc.
Malta, NY

*See, I have placed
before you an open door
that no one can shut.
Rev 3:8*

Open Door Publishers, Inc
P.O. Box 2319
Malta, NY 12020 (518) 899-2097
http://www.opendoorpublishers.com

Printed in the United States of America

First Edition

ISBN: 978-0-9841721-8-4

For my parents, with love,
and to EVERY girl in the world
who has ever felt "NOT" good enough.
GIRLPOWER! Pass It on. . .

Je m'appelle SABRINA

Sabrina Davis walked into her apartment that night to the familiar smell of coffee grounds and Vanilla Musk, her newest Target fragrance discovery. It was what her friends affectionately referred to as "stripper perfume" but she loved the sweet, spicy scent and hint of vanilla. It made her feel slightly glamorous and sexy and God knows she was desperate for some sort of skip in her step. If Vanilla Musk provided the skip, so be it.

Sabrina stood in the darkness and took a deep breathe as she felt the busyness of her day turn into a quiet silence. At 33 years old with absolutely no sign of love on the horizon, she stood in the stillness that felt peaceful yet heavy with the unknown. The stillness seemed to sigh with Sabrina and strangely, this dark stillness was somehow a comfort to Sabrina, as if to whisper, "You are not alone, I am with you."

Its not that Sabrina didn't have dates or offers for romantic dinners. In fact, she had more than a few offers. She was in great shape, had popping bright eyes, a personality that was charming, vivacious, yet deep, and wise beyond her years. From the outside, she had it all, a booming private counseling practice, a wonderful close-knit family full of love and a tight-knit group of friends that made her laugh and were true and loyal. She did have it all, but something deep inside her longed for love. It wasn't that Sabrina wanted so much someone to love her, as she was ready to share her love with the right one. The last few years Sabrina was consumed with graduate school for counseling and building her own private practice.

While most of her girlfriends were falling in love and planning their weddings, Sabrina was planning her career. She was far from ready to be in a committed relationship, and frankly she felt she barely had a handle on her own life, let alone meshing it with someone else's. The thought of cooking and being domestic with someone terrified her and actually made her feel like her throat was closing. For a long time, Sabrina felt like she was the only woman she knew that wasn't rushing to the altar or baby land. As the youngest of four and having had two sisters marry early and start their families, Sabrina knew she wanted to plunge into building a career she was passionate about. There was, however, one love that Sabrina actually considered taking the plunge with.

Sabrina graduated from grad school and headed to The City to move in with her friend, Marley. She got a job counseling cancer patients, and it was there that she met Josh. Josh was a genius scientist who worked in the hospital lab where Sabrina counseled patients. He had the widest brown eyes you have ever laid eyes on and dimples so adorable they could make you remove your clothes immediately. After months of shameless flirting and banter, Josh finally asked her to dinner. Countless dinners, vodka tonics and heavy make out sessions (great kisser by the way), Sabrina fell madly in love and was SURE this was it. Sort of. Almost positive.

You see, something deep within her insides knew that if she married Josh that she would slowly begin to sacrifice parts of herself to keep him happy and their marriage alive. Josh was a genius scientist that spent every waking moment in the lab. Sabrina was a therapist who thrived on connecting people and their hearts. Often times she would plea for him to leave the lab so they could spend time together, to which he would always object and postpone for the almighty lab. He also hated fur and refused to eat veal. Sabrina loved fur and ate steak as if it were the last supper. He preferred the *Times* and political debates, while Sabrina indulged in the latest gossip magazines and could debate for hours whether TomKat would make it or break it. He found her lack of attention to world issues shallow and caddy. She found his need for constant intellectual stimulation boring and stiff. Yet despite these obvious differences, they shared a sense of humor that led to a chemistry so intense she would sometimes have to pinch herself. Josh could make her laugh in a way no other had even come close. They would spend hours in hysterics over the silliest of things. But as the relationship wore on their differences became insurmountable. As they tried to bridge the gap one thing became increasingly clear.

Josh thought Sabrina was intellectually vacant. He told her she would never be able to be the intellectual companion he needed. Sabrina was devastated. She began to question her intellect and feel inferior to Josh and all his geeky lab friends. So what if she wore a pink puffy coat to survive the winters. So what if she preferred cabs to public transportation. She would only realize after the break up that she was who she was and that was enough. But the self doubt set in, and she became engulfed in a deep depression of self doubt and shame. Maybe she should read the *Times* more and stop wearing fur. Maybe she ought to "grow up" whatever the hell that meant.

Those months after the break up were filled with lonely nights and streams of tears. Some days, she found it difficult to get out bed and face the day. Every place she went was a reminder of their love affair, and Sabrina found herself losing her sparkle and pizzazz for life. It was then that she decided to move home near her family and work with her mother in private practice. She missed them dearly and felt that this is what she needed to shake out of her slump. Bags packed and tearful good-byes to her friends and she was home bound.

HOME. Always a place of love, acceptance and laughter. Home to the people that allowed her to wear her big puffy pink coat and spend hours reading *People* and *Us*. Home to the place where she could be who she was and feel the love and support of her family. She felt a sigh of relief well up as she began the next chapter of her life.

Those first few months were just what she needed. She moved in with her parents, spent time with her family, reconnected with childhood friends and began to get the spark back in her step. Her practice began to thrive and she was finally becoming comfortable again in her own skin. Until the e-mail. The dreaded e-mail:

Dear Sabrina,

As hard as it is for me to write this I am sure its even harder for you to read (arrogant jerk!!! Why harder for me! Sabrina thinks).

Shelly and I are engaged and will be getting married next year. I wanted to tell you over the phone but lost your number.

Be well, Josh.

Gulp. Gasp. Puke. OMG OMG OMG. The only man I have ever loved in my entire life is getting married and it's not to me, thought Sabrina.

The beauty of working with her mom was that she could always run into her office in times of need. Sabrina flew down the hall and practically crashed through the door. She flung herself into her mother's wing chair and did the ugly cry/wail. "MOM!!!!!!!! HE'S GETTING MARRIED! And she recycles, loves the *Times* and is concerned, deeply concerned with global warming."

Dear Josh,

Fuck off and be miserable for the rest of your life without me.

In lust, Sabrina

Dear Josh,

I have a big fur coat and a veal farm where I slaughter calves for fun.

Xoxo, Sabrina

Dear Josh,

I am not stupid. In fact I am really smart, smart enough to know any guy who questions my intelligence is an arrogant prick.

In Genius, Sabrina

(Be the bigger person, Sabrina thinks. Write from your heart.)

Dear Josh,

You were my first love and will be in my heart forever. I wish you and Nature Girl a wonderful life together full of beautiful babies, laughter, prosperity and green house gas solutions.

Love, Sabrina.

No more Josh. No hope of ever being together. Days of listening to tragic love songs and reviewing every detail of their relationship slowly came to an end, and Sabrina healed her broken heart. She came to the realization that she had much more growing to do before she would be ready for marriage. And while her heart hurt at the thought of Josh building his life with someone else, she knew deep down they were not meant for a lifetime.

Life progressed and Sabrina threw herself into her practice. She started volunteering with a local camp for at-risk youth.

It was there that she met Phil. What could she say about Phil? A talented founder of a Non-Profit group for at-risk youth who had a gift for working with kids and a huge dazzling smile that lit up the room. Sabrina admired him and his passion for his work and enthusiasm for life. She found herself glued to his every word.

Sabrina started running support groups for him, and while she should have been in her genius therapist mode, she could barely focus on the tasks at hand. Every time Phil was near her, she felt a jolt of electricity. The kind that makes you feel like you're going to throw up, scream and pee your pants from the over excitement. She was attracted to everything about him and felt a pull toward him. There was no denying he felt the same, and she knew it was only a matter of time before he asked her out.

One evening when Sabrina had finished running one of the groups, Phil taped a card on her windshield asking her to dinner and boom, that was it. They started an intense romance of long evening make out sessions. The kind that makes you feel like you're seventeen and the world will come to an end if you don't get to make out with your boyfriend, in this case, Phil. He was funny, smart and attractive in a major dork-like quality. Ever since dating the lab geek, Sabrina found herself lusting after dorks.

Only problem with dear sweet Phil was that, behind closed doors he was outgoing and hysterical but the minute they went out in public or spent time with other people, Phil became another person. Shy, awkward and intensely silent. So awkward in fact that Sabrina felt certain he had an identical twin brother that abducted Phil and locked him in the closet. Where was hysterical fun Phil? Had his identical twin abducted his personality or no, was it worse than that.

"Ohhh no," thought Sabrina. It couldn't be, Sabrina realized the hard core truth. Phil was an ego maniac. She had read about them in grad school. You know the type, it's all about feeding the ego, and anytime poor old Phil felt like Sabrina's attention was elsewhere, he became like a small stubborn child waiting for her affection and attention. Goodbye Phil. Case closed. Diagnosis: EGO-MANIAC.

As the new year approached, Sabrina threw herself into her practice and began to enjoy her life. She was finally making enough money to get her own place and let's face it, 30 living with your parents isn't exactly the catch of the year. So with excitement and hope, she settled in to her new gorgeous apartment in the heart of the city. She loved it. With granite counter tops and black sheik appliances, Sabrina felt like Carrie Bradshaw, except no Mr. Big.

Just Mr. Insecure, Mr. Arrogant, Mr. Mamma's boy, Mr. Socially Handicapped, Mr. Fashionably Challenged (hint: Mom jeans, GAG), Mr. Oh, excuse me, wait, drum roll please....its DR. Narcissist. And in case you are wondering, under no circumstances will he give you free medical advice. This was made very clear to Sabrina when her dear friend, Preppy, asked the Doc for some guidance. "Tell YOUR friends to call my secretary and don't ever put me in that situation again." Ouch.

Come on Sabrina say it, "You are an arrogant prick who has no idea what love is, and you will forever be alone, and even when surrounded by love, you are too blind to see it, know it, feel it, receive it, or keep it, and I feel so sorry for you because you will forever, for the rest of your life, if you choose, and I pray to God you won't, be DR. Narcissist."

Nope, Sabrina couldn't spit the words out. Instead, she took a bubble bath. Later she would wonder if that was because he made her feel ashamed and she was attempting to wash the shame away. But in the end, Sabrina knew the truth. It took courage to love well and be true. Maybe, he just wasn't there yet. Hopefully, he got there. And on to the last category there was Mr. Gay. Had to be. Loved fashion and Broadway musicals, a sure tell sign.

She was on the dating circuit and hating it. Where was Mr. True Love? Where was an instant chemistry and unspoken connection that would last forever? He was late. Very late. And she was approaching 34 and totally single. Tragically single. Smile on her face, new dress and pink frosted lipstick. Forever the third wheel, we have someone for you, how can you be single, your so beautiful and smart? Attention please, Sabrina wanted to shout, Single by choice! Not willing to settle. Not willing for one more minute to be with rather than without. No she was fine with it. Really. Totally happy. Totally at peace. Totally okay. I AM OKAY. Gulp. Was it her? Was she too picky? Would anyone ever get her humor and quirky personality?

She and her best friend from childhood, Kat, would spend hours debating this over Coronas and Marlboro lights. Good old Kat. The forever loyal true friend that Sabrina could not live without. Stable strong steady Kat. "Its so not YOU. He's just stupid, insecure, arrogant, or gay." That was the newest and favorite category. "You weren't rejected, he's just gay." Right. Poor guy. Hope he finds happiness someday with the man of his dreams.

Kat was the type of friend who was always there when Sabrina would begin to question herself. Together they had survived the high school years of survival of the fittest. Their friendship had grown into one of depth and love, an unspoken bond that connected their hearts. Kat was her sounding board for it all.

So as she stood in her empty apartment, she felt a strange peace that was becoming increasingly comfortable. Sabrina was finally settling into this alone thing. Somewhere deep inside, she knew love would make its way toward her. She knew it was coming and had all the faith in the world that it would be true love. And for now she was really okay on her own.

As she turned on the stereo and poured a glass of wine, she began getting ready for the evening. Kat and her close friend, Fashionista were on their way over to spend the summer evening on her terrace. Fashionista-a gorgeous, tall girl with a flighty creative personality. Fashionista could walk into any room and have all eyes on her. But the best thing about this gorgeous creature is she didn't even pay attention to it. She was a genuine girl who loved good friends, fine wine and FASHION. Sabrina loved her carefree spirit and love of life.

This was going to be a good old fashioned girls night. Wine, cigs, (and yes, Sabrina was aware of the dangers of smoking and vowed to quit before her next birthday. Swear on Vanilla Musk), and her favorite mix of... Michael Jackson, Stevie Wonder, and dear ol' Sinatra all rolled into one.

As she got ready for the evening, she carefully applied her frosted pink lipstick. Her brother's girlfriend, Chloe, had begged her to trade the frost in for clear natural gloss. Fashionista had even staged a pink frost protest, but Sabrina couldn't shake it. There was just something about that damn frosty glimmer that she was addicted to. As she danced around her apartment and got dressed, she heard her very pink phone (to match her lipstick of course) ring. She loved her ring. It was a new age chime ensemble that made her feel like she should fall into downward dog and say NAMASTE.

"Smith!"

"Hi Doll." Smith was an old friend. Really old. Like twenty years older old. A big wig accountant with a passion and fondness for younger women. Like not yet born younger. The running joke was the Future X Mrs. Smith has not yet been born. While Smith and Sabrina shared a great chemistry and had loads of fun bantering, the line was drawn. Friend zone forever.

Smith: What are you wearing? (Typical Smith.)

Sabrina: You are sick and twisted.

Smith: Ah Davis, you know me well.

Sabrina: Getting ready for girls night, no dirty old men allowed.

Smith: Damn it, Davis.

Sabrina: Sorry, maybe heading to Aberdeen later. Will call if you want to meet us out. I think they have a senior citizen discount.

Smith: Drop dead Davis.

Sabrina: You will before me Smith.

Click. Sabrina smiled to herself. She had such gratitude for the friends she had collected since moving home. Loyal, hysterical and brilliant. She felt blessed to have such a close knit group of pals. She searched through her closet deciding on jeans and a Target fitted trendy Tee. Target was her new best friend. She could find dresses that passed for designer. Last summer a girl stopped her on the street to ask if her wrap dress was Gucci. Sabrina laughed. Mossimo Merona-only at Target. NOOOO, the girl gasped. Ohhhhhhh-hhhh yes, this season.

As she got dressed and finished her make up she felt excited about the night to come. This was the unveiling of Phoebe Blueblood. George's new fiancé. George Countryclub. Sabrina and George had been on and off since the 8th grade and tragically addicted to each other. George unavailable=Sabrina chases him. Sabrina unavailable=George chases her. Fifteen years of tumultuous on and off again. George began calling Sabrina last winter only to come to the conclusion that she was the one, the only girl for him. Sabrina had been waiting for this revelation. George and Sabrina=TLF (true love forever). Wait. Re do. Should read TFU (totally fucked up). But Sabrina was curious and hopeful and willing to give it a shot. So George flew into town to whisk her off her feet, until he went to the bathroom that is.

"You should get a new bathrobe, that one is sooooo ratty and old." Note to self: buy new sexy bathrobe effective immediately. Why couldn't she say: note to self, you are a fucking asshole. Sabrina was getting weary of constantly altering herself for the sake of pleasing men. It was exhausting. Not long after the bathrobe it was her nails. You should really grow your nails. Shit. He caught her. Nail picker, former nail biter, transitioned to nail picker. Baby steps. Little did George Countryclub know she used to chew on Barbie shoes as well, but thank God there were none lurking in her apartment. That was one addiction she had broken free of for good.

Seven years old, at the kitchen table surrounded by her very loving parents, sisters and brother. "Sabrina, you really must stop biting your nails. You are about to enter the first grade, and we, as your loving, adoring family, refuse to let you enter the first grade if you continue down this self destructive path of NAIL BITING."

"Fine" Sabrina says sternly. "It's Finished" (let them eat cake…) but as all good and true genius therapists know, while you can call someone out on their addiction, in her case, nail biting, the addict, without treatment, will quickly replace one addiction for another.

Fine, no more nail biting ever. But here was the replacement, Barbie shoes. Sabrina loved Barbie Shoes, the cold hard plastic feel between her teeth, Ahhhh DELICIOUS. And more than Barbie shoes, Sabrina loved Barbie legs, but not the plastic kind, they were too hard, no way, she was an old school Barbie's legs made of rubber kind of girl. And while every girl had Rodeo Barbie, Nightclub Barbie, Career Barbie…. Sabrina's Barbies had turned into, with her help of course, "Childhood Polio Barbie" because darling sweet Sabrina, no matter how hard she tried to resist, would chew their feet, sometimes even ankles, to get her fix.

And then one day Sabrina was invited to Sally Simple's, her next door neighbor, to play Barbies. Sabrina was too embarrassed to bring her collection of Polio Barbies so she came empty handed. As they played, Sally Simple brought out the true kryptonite of all, beautiful, perfectly pink, with a shade of lavender, brand spanking new, never worn, Barbie shoes. And Sabrina drooled and felt a deep burning compulsion start to burn in her heart.

"NOOO, SABRINA," she said to herself. "UNDER NO CIRCUMSTANCES CAN YOU EAT THESE SHOES," but it was too late.

Sally Simple had innocently headed to the bathroom. And while every bone in her 7-year old body told her not to do it, Sabrina grabbed these glorious perfectly pink with a hint of lavender shoes and put them in her mouth and chewed and AHHH it was delicious, hard brand new, never touched, crispy Barbie shoes in her mouth delicious.

Then, Sabrina heard the toilet flush, and as every addict does, reality soon set in, and Sabrina realized what she had done. She spit the glorious best Barbie shoes ever out of her mouth and stared at the remnants. Little tiny pieces fell into her hands. And with that, evidence in hand, Sabrina ran for the door, skipped over the fence, and charged the back screen door that was called HOME. She quickly threw away the evidence and forever would live with the guilt of having chewed up, and literally spit out, Sally Simple's brand new Barbie shoes.

Dear Sally Simple,

Sabrina Davis, your former neighbor, here. I did it. I ate, chewed and maybe even secretly, but not so secretly anymore, savored ever minute of chewing up your gorgeous brand new delicious perfectly pink, with a hint of lavender, Barbie Shoes.

Please forgive me. I swear for the last twenty five years I have been in search for a replacement pair. Please don't hate me forever.

Sincerely, Sabrina "I chew on Barbie shoes" Davis.

Now as an adult, George Countryclub, was calling Sabrina out on her nail picking (former nail biting, turned to Barbie shoe chewing, settled into nail picking) addiction. She looked at her nails and felt a slow rise of shame build. What she should have felt was anger. Anger that this asshole was being a control freak. Instead, she made a note to have a manicure that week. Ratty bathrobe, short nails, quickly turned into Your tooo spiritual, tooo emotional, tooo outgoing, tooo confident....translation too YOU. Ohhh, so that was the problem. It was her. And then Poof. George dropped off the face of the earth. Weeks went on and he stopped calling. When he did call it was a 5 AM pub crawl home with slurry messages of love and lust.

Then the news broke. Kat called to say George Countryclub had met Phoebe Blueblood and they were engaged. I should have gotten a new robe, Sabrina thought. And grown my nails. And be an atheist. Game over. Another one bites the dust. And faithful and true Kat did what she does best. HE MUST BE GAY. Or, just not that into you, but the code was to never ever admit that he just wasn't that into her.

Sabrina bounced back quickly and she and Kat came to the conclusion that she had been saved from a life of control and sheer boredom. Sabrina felt relieved that she and Georgie were FINALLY over. But secretly Sabrina wondered what did Phoebe Blueblood have that she didn't? Tonight, she was about to find out. Kat had been invited to their engagement party, and Sabrina knew Kat would innocently get plenty of pictures of Phoebe Blueblood.

Tonight was the night of unveiling. No longer would Sabrina have to wonder who this creature was. She felt the anticipation of the night build and soon the terrace was filled with wine, Sinatra, and the envelope.

"Ok," Kat said, "here it is." Sabrina wanted to bite her nails in the moment of truth, but resisted as this could have been the reason Phoebe was in the picture and she wasn't. Heart thumping. Dry mouth. Here we go…drum roll please…… "Phoebe Blueblood."

Hours of analysis and wine later, Sabrina was relieved. Phoebe Blueblood was no match for her. Sabrina was thinner and more beautiful. Every girl's dream, to be thinner than the one he left you for. Phew. Phoebe clearly had not gotten the memo: CARBS ARE NOT YOUR FRIEND. But she did have long nails. And probably a brand new robe.

Although Sabrina was pleased at the victory, deep down she felt sorry for Phoebe Blueblood. George Countryclub was unable to love or accept anyone most of all himself. Every girl deserved to be with the knight in shining armor, and George was the knight in every country club. This was his life's ambition. To be in every club imaginable. Poor innocent Phoebe Blueblood. Sabrina realized this girl had no idea what she was in for and instead of feeling grateful she was thinner she was feeling sad for Phoebe Blueblood. Deep down Sabrina knew she had no idea what she was in for with George, and she couldn't help but honor true girl code which states, in case you don't know "EVERY GIRL DESERVES TO BE TO-TALLY ADORED AND ACCEPTED." Pass it on.

As the last of the wine was poured, the verdict was out, and the girls were headed to Aberdeen. The summer spot where any-one who's anyone gathered. Large outside terrace, great margaritas, music and lots of eye candy. Funny though, Sabrina wasn't even thinking about the eye candy. She was simply enjoying the moment and taking it all in. Girlfriends. The best girlfriends. This is what it's about, Sabrina thought to herself.

"That's it!" exclaimed Fashionista. "You are not going out like that!!! Show me to your closet."

What's wrong with Mossimo Merona?? Sabrina thought to herself. With glee Fashionista began crafting the ultimate outfit for Sabrina. Yelling out orders to Sabrina to show her skinniest, tightest jeans, and then wala-a scarf. The scarf. Sabrina had a scarf collection given to her by her grandmother. As Fashionista poured through the collection she grabbed a turquoise and white Hermes scarf that was stunning. Sabrina stared totally confused. Summer. Hot. Scarf??

"Take off your shirt and bra," Fashionista ordered. Yes Ma'am done. Within seconds Fashionista had created a top for Sabrina that was the scarf, tied in the back to reveal most of her back.

"Heels please."

"Okay, ok," said Sabrina starting to feel herself break a sweat from Fashionista's bossy personality. Strappy summer heels, gold hoops, gold bangles, skinny jeans, hot scarf, and to finish off, frosted pink lipstick, OF COURSE.

"Turn around!" gushed Fashionista.

"OMG!!!" yelled Kat. And that is when Sabrina saw her reflection in the mirror. HOT. Totally completely HOT. She had been called cute, maybe even beautiful but never HOT.

She stared at the reflection looking back and gasped, "I AM HOT!"

"TOTALLY!" screamed Kat as Fashionista smiled at her creation. Sabrina suddenly felt a strange confidence began to rise. She felt the on FIRE I AM GORGEOUS HOT. And they all agreed. George Countryclub who????? I am HOT. WHO CARES?????? And with that they were off for an unforgettable night. Sabrina had no idea what was about to happen. She was too busy feeling HOT.

HOTTIE FRATATTI

As they approached Aberdeen, they could hear the sounds of music and laughter. A hot steamy night with nothing but good music and margaritas to look forward to. Sabrina could not stop smiling and as she walked in she noticed every male eye upon the trio. So this is what it's like to be HOT, she thought. She had never felt like this before, but strangely, she had no interest in talking to eye candy, or even flirting for that matter. She was completely content to be with her best girlfriends, enjoy the music and the margaritas.

"CHARLIE" Sabrina yelled. It was Charlie, an acquaintance she knew who ran with the local political crowd.

"HEY Sabrina, ladies, what's going on?"

"Just enjoying the summer night," Sabrina yelled over the music.

"Great, just finished a business dinner. What can I get you guys?"

"Margaritas!" they shouted in unison.

Sabrina began to sway her hips to the beat and dance with a carefree attitude. Totally free, totally confident, totally HOT. Sabrina had never felt this feeling before. This feeling of contentment, confidence, peace and feminine POWER. She could barely believe that she was finally in a place where she didn't care that she was single. In fact, that night, she didn't even entertain the thought of talking to the male species. Charlie returned and they quickly finished their drinks.

"I'm up next," yelled Sabrina. As she walked to the bar she stood tall and focused on trying to get through the crowd. Drinks in hand she turned to head back to the table and that's when she saw HIM.

Their eyes locked on one another and Sabrina felt as if time had literally stopped. In one moment the earth had stopped rotating and she was completely still and stunned. He looked directly at her with deep brown soulful eyes and a killer smile. "Hi," he said.

"Hi," said Sabrina suddenly conscious of how she looked. She slowly put her hair behind her ear and took a deep breathe. In a split second she felt something deep within, a spark and force she had never experienced. Could it be? Love at first sight? Keep walking, her feet shouted. But her eyes were glued on him. He was gorgeous. Hot. Hottie. Deep brown huge eyes and dark hair with specks of gray. Her absolute favorite. Legs unsteady she kept walking only to hear him laugh behind her.

"I am not following you, just heading to my friend's table." Sabrina pretended to ignore him secretly hoping he was about to pass out at the sight of her exposed back. Thank GOD for Fashionista. As she headed back to the table he was there. Behind her. With Charlie. OMG. He was with Charlie. This hot hot HOTTIE guy was going to sit at their table. Be cool Sabrina. Rules. Remember the rules. Do not lock eyes, do not ignore your girlfriends, and do not talk too much. Right. Rules. On it. Shit. He was staring at her. Totally locked in. And she loved it. He sat down next to her. Breathe Sabrina. And that was it. Eyes locked, girlfriends ignored, talking incessantly they were engulfed in one another. Sabrina had never ever felt anything remotely close to this. At first moment she wanted more, more closeness more talk more, more, more. Shit Sabrina. Don't do this. You are content. You are peaceful. You are okay being single.

HE IS TOTALLY HOT AND TONIGHT YOU ARE TOTAL-LY HOT SO GO FOR IT! And that was when true girl code took over. This was the part where Kat would interrogate the fresh hot meat, and Sabrina would sit back downloading the information preparing for their morning debrief over coffee in which they would analyze Hottie and his life story over and over and over again. They had this down to a science. Kat was the very happily, married mother of a gorgeous baby girl, innocent best friend out for a good time, and Sabrina was the observer taking it all in.

It would be too obvious if Sabrina had asked the questions and darling Kat knew the time had come to go in for the kill. Get all stats immediately to assess whether this is a potential catch for Sabrina. Hottie is 40, big attorney for a major corporation well known for its ability to make shit loads of money going after corrupt corporations. Corporate. Suit. Delicious suit. Amazing tie.

This was all too good to be true. And sure enough, it was. Gasp. Pause. There they were…no it couldn't be, he was too hot, too gorgeous, too successful. Sad but true. PLEATS. Big waist gapping pleats. Oh Dear God, Sabrina thought. Citizens arrest here and now. Pleats are illegal for potential soul mate. Hello, fashion hell called, they want their pleats back. She should have walked away at that moment, but as all girls do, she was secretly excited. A potential fashion makeover! Imagine being the woman who weans him off of pleats forever.

This was too intoxicating for Sabrina to process. And there was Kat, interrogating Hot fresh meat. The information kept coming, attorney, had an apartment nearby, separated. PAUSE. Record skips. WHAT???? Separated. Marriage ending. Ten-year old daughter…And pleats. NOOOOOOOOO, thought Sabrina. This was a cruel joke. The hottest, gorgeous, most charming, electrifying man she had ever laid eyes on was separated with a child. Didn't she just see this on Oprah? Never ever go out with a guy in the separation phase. Too much baggage. Too much drama. Sabrina felt devastatingly disappointed.

An ambitious, gorgeous guy and 40 years old, her most favorite age. At 40 most men were either fucked up for life or had had the epiphany of truth where they know what they want out of life and are determined to get it. So here he was, well dressed (minus pleats) in the murky category of somewhat available, but not completely. Oh Noo, the GRAY zone, and gray by the way was Sabrina's LEAST favorite color.

But why was he staring at her? And why was she enamored from the second they locked eyes? It's the damn scarf Sabrina thought to herself. You're just having a lusty summer night and this is flirting. Nothing substantial, nothing to worry about. Just flirting. But why did she feel so close to him? Why did she feel electricity when their legs touched under the table? Margaritas, it had to be the damn tequila. Besides, he wears pleats. Puh Lease! But deep down she KNEW this was different. Way different. Shit, she thought, I so should have gotten acrylic nails and a new robe.

As the night drew to a close, Kat insisted on the late night stop for pizza. Sabrina in her new found hotness knew that carbs were not her friend (she had gotten the memo). No way was she going to risk her slowly shrinking body for a late night binge.There they were about to say goodbye when Sabrina broke all the rules. "Walk me home," she said, alarmingly assertive to Hottie. He looked at her with eager anticipation and quickly replied how about a ride home instead.

This is the part where logic should take over, and Sabrina knew she should run. Run, fast and hard. But it was too late, she was in deep. Plus she wasn't about to run in heels. Really nice heels that she loved and made her toes look adorable. Hottie had abducted her brain and taken over with his charm and devastatingly gorgeous smile. As they ascended the hill toward Main Street he pointed to his car, and, that my friends is when she knew she was in trouble. Big trouble. Capital T!!!!! TROUBLE. At that moment, God Himself opened up the skies as she laid eyes on the most beautiful creature she had ever seen. Cherry Red convertible Ferrari. I repeat FERRARI. Oh nooooooo!

Dear God:

Sabrina Davis here. Don't you know that hot boys and fast cars make me vulnerable to a night full of sinful lust??????????????? (No answer. Great, probably working on the gas crisis. Hope He checks His voice mail.)

Okay Sabrina, what would you tell a client? Run for the hills, do not pass go, do not collect two hundred dollars, just fucking run (even if you are in heels)!

What would you tell a friend? Go for it! You need this, you want this. What do you have to lose? This is it, go go go enjoy, devour HIM! Great. Head saying run. Body pleading to stay. Feet paralyzed in indecision. And that my friends, is when the decision was made. Sabrina caught a glimpse of herself in the reflection of the shiny bright red car and knew that was her kryptonite. She could not live with herself if she didn't have a ride in this car with the ultimate Hottie. She was attracted to everything about him. He was ambitious and driven, yet light and real. The damn smile was making her weak in the knees.

"Here we are," he said, staring at her with the deep brown eyes. The eyes that seemed to know everything about her without knowing a thing. They were mesmerizing. As he opened the car door she suddenly realized there was no turning back. All rules broken. No running away. No hiding from his gaze. She was getting in. Getting in for the joy ride of her life.

As they cruised down Main Street, GIMMEE SHELTER by the Rolling Stones filled the summer air. Sabrina sang along and secretly wished that anyone who had ever crossed her in any way was witnessing this miracle. HOT GIRL, IN HOT CAR, WITH HOT GUY. EAT MY DUST. ATTENTION EX BOYFRIENDS -YOUR LOSS!! Hair flowing, heart pounding, eyes wide, Sabrina was in a daze. I WILL NOT SLEEP WITH THIS MAN. Mental check, did not shave legs, have granny underwear on. Phew. Sabrina was practicing safe sex.

Every girl knew the surest way to protect yourself from indiscretion was to throw away your razor and wear Hanes Her Way. The kind with the huge waistband that said HANES all along the border. Why was she suddenly wishing she had pulled the tag from her sexy Victoria's Secret underwear? Sabrina's secret: I will not, under any circumstances, swear on my unshaven legs, period underwear and dead grandmother's scarf, sleep with this man.

As they walked into her apartment for a night cap she suddenly panicked. Where did she leave her various nasal sprays and were there any super overnighter with wings pads lurking? Too late now. She turned on the Sinatra, he opened the wine and they headed to the terrace where they quickly fell into a comfortable rhythm. They talked and talked and talked for hours.

Every time she looked into his eyes she felt a jolt. What kind of a jolt she wasn't quite sure. All she knew was that this was a feeling she had never, ever, in her life had. A strange comfort and familiarity as if she had known him forever. She tried to shake the feeling and pass it off but it wouldn't budge. He was different. Way different than any man she had ever met. He was like her. Ambitious and driven in his career, funny and charming, deeply loyal and mind blowing hysterical. She had met her match. Someone like HER!!!!!!!!!!!!!!!

Easy girl. Slow down. Remember, you did not shave your legs and your underwear is hideous. But it was too late, he leaned in close, took her face in his hands gently and sweetly, Oh God, it was really happening, kissed her. A slow gentle sweet kiss…then began the transition to passionate, yearning, I can't live without you. You're the hottest smartest most wonderful girl in the whole world Sabrina kiss. (And I don't care that you eat meat, wear fur, have a ratty bathrobe and pick, but used to bite, your nails.) The most unbelievable kiss she had ever had. That song, that stupid song *It's in His Kiss*, so this is what they were talking about…"if you wanna know if he loves you so it's in his kiss"…Slowly the kiss moves from the terrace to the living room.

Sabrina: It's late, you should go.

Hottie: Right it's late, I should go.
Kiss. Embrace. Heavy catholic appropriate petting.
Hottie: I'm not leaving.
Sabrina: I know.

Make out city. The best kissing she ever experienced. Movie kissing. Where were the cameras?? Someone needed to witness this. Sabrina needed proof that she and Hottie were the new Sahottie. (Sabrina + Hottie combined, refer to Bennifer, Tomkat or Brangelina).

Morning comes far too quickly, and Sabrina awakens to find Hottie staring at her. "You my dear are adorable." OMG. Hot and adorable all in the same night. Need this on tape, please repeat. Sabrina felt herself float to the ceiling. His eyes were literally taking her in inch by inch. And guess what, in tact, clothes on discretion maintained. Thank God for Hanes.

"So, when can I see you again?" Gulp.

Definitely will have to shave and remove tags from sexy underwear. "Well," Sabrina replied, "I am heading to the beach this week for a vacation with my family. I'll be back next weekend."

"Great," Hottie says. "How is next Saturday, dinner?" Definitely shaving and waxing chin hair that keeps cropping up. Oh and remove all nasal sprays and pads from the premises. And starve self at beach and get really tan, but not face, don't want wrinkles.

"Great, next Saturday." Hot passionate embrace. Make out city. Best kiss of her life. She was screwed. Big time. As the door shut Sabrina grabbed her phone and speed dialed Kat. She answered on the first ring.

Kat: Did you see the pleats?
Sabrina: Heartbreaking.
Kat: He looks like he has a great body but the pleats made him look fat.
Sabrina: Gasp. I KNOW!!!
Kat: Very cool guy, he could not take his eyes off you.

Sabrina: I KNOW! It was intense.

Kat: So, did you know?

Sabrina: God no, but let's put it this way, thank God for un-shaven legs and bad underwear.

Kat: Close call. So, seeing him again?

Sabrina: Will see, supposed to go out when I get back from the beach.

Kat: Awesome you will be tan and relaxed.

Sabrina: I know there's just something about him...

Kat: Baby crying, gotta run. Have fun at the beach!

Sabrina: K, thanks for the interrogation and please Google him.

Kat: Got it. Hottie Fratatti right?

Sabrina: Roger, I want a full report.

Kat: Done. On it.

Click. This is the thing about having a best friend. They always have your back. Willing to interrogate, cross examine, and do a background check to make sure you will never ever under any circumstances, be hurt again. Kat was her best friend, her true wing woman. Sabrina felt a deep comfort knowing that Kat knew her better than anyone, maybe even better than she knew herself. More than that, Sabrina knew Kat was on his trail. Hottie Fratatti was under full investigation pleats and all.

Sipping her coffee and throwing her bikini into a duffle bag Sabrina felt very strange. Excited, nervous and strangely intrigued. Who was... Hottie Fratatti, and why was he imprinted in her mind?

B each week. Every year the family traveled down to Delaware to lie in the sun, laugh and eat. Big problem, Sabrina could not eat. Hottie Fratatti was there, every moment, every minute, seeping into her mind and body. Love or lust? Not sure yet, but the thought of food was making her nauseous. Who could eat having seen the most beautiful long eyelashes and deep brown eyes of Hottie? Food was unimaginable. And then there was the damn linger of his touch upon her face. It was as if his fingers were programmed to know exactly what Sabrina wanted. Slow, lingering, gentle, but not too gentle. Just the right mix of passion and purity. How the hell was she going to get through this week with Hottie Fratatti lingering everywhere?

Unpacked. Sunscreen on and headed to the beach for a day of total sun and relaxation. Phone chimes. Text message. It's Hottie.

Hottie: I miss and want you.

Sabrina: What do you miss and what do you want?

Hottie: Your lips. Your eyes. Your body. YOU.

(Gasp. OMG. Beach. Family. Steamy texts. Sabrina blushes and hopes her family will think it's the heat.)

Sabrina: Can't wait to see you. All of you.

Hottie: Miss you like crazy. Counting down the minutes. WHO ARE YOU SABRINA DAVIS? I cannot get my mind off you?????

Sabrina: Just wait and see. You have only scratched the surface.

Hottie: Can't wait, DARLING.

OMG. Darling. 8 years old, favorite show Hart to Hart. Meet Jennifer and Jonathan Hart. The glamorous, oh so attractive couple, who were private investigators. Sabrina grew up on this show and had always pretended to be Jennifer Hart, aka Stefanie Powers, aka

DARLING. As a little girl she would dress up and pretend to be Jonathan's Darling. Smart, sophisticated, sexy, Darling. How did Hottie Fratatti know? Oh shit, Sabrina thought. Hottie called her darling. This might be true love status. Never in the history of Sabrina Davis had she been called Darling.

Dear Jonathan and Jennifer Hart,

Loved your show. Especially the beginning when you guys drive in the yellow convertible Mercedes Benz along the coast of CA. I thought you were both very talented professional detectives. By the way, loved the butler, Max, but since I have allergies, I was never a big fan of the dog. And just so you know, my life goal was to have a relationship like yours. Hot, passionate, loyal and true. I think I might have met him. His name is Hottie Fratatti and he calls me Darling. Did you get that D-A-R-L-I-N-G?

Much love and thanks for inspiring me to love with abandon, Sabrina aka DARLING Davis

As Sabrina soaked in the rays and enjoyed the sound of the waves, Lucy, her fourteen-year old niece handed her the other ear piece to her iPod. They sang along to the music and flipped thru the latest issues of *Teen Beat*. That's right, you read it right. 33years old and scrolling thru *Teen Beat* to see if she could get any information on the opening of *High School Musical 3, Senior Year*. She could not wait. And secretly or not so secretly now, Sabrina loved *High School Musical*. She even cried during 1 and 2. Practically hysterical at the end of the first one when they sing "We're All in This Together…" She would keep it on the Disney Station on XM just to be able to hear it once and while.

And here's the deal, its not that she was an immature teenie bopper longing for her high school years. It was the overall message, its okay to be you, to be different, to be proud of who you are because the truth is "WE ARE ALL IN THIS TOGETHER."

Her high school years were nothing like that. It was constant fear at any minute you could go from the top of the food chain to the bottom in the blink of an eye. Filled with anxiety, she had wished she had the group of friends Troy and Gabriella had. Instead it was full of slander, exposing your deepest insecurities and constant sarcasm. Why couldn't Sabrina have felt like Gabriella? Peaceful in who she was always following her heart. Well for one, it IS a Disney movie, but maybe the truth was this is unacceptable in the most popular chain and anyone who ever did "Follow their Heart" lived in Loserville. No way could you be vulnerable, the minute you were, you were out. Gone. Fighting your way back in every step of the way.

Sabrina found herself watching beautiful, wise beyond her years, Lucy, who was so confident and unafraid. Not obsessing about how she looked or what she said. Just happy to be herself and knowing that she was as Lucy would agree, "FABULOUS."

What Lucy didn't know is that Sabrina was watching, taking it all in, and practicing that kind of confidence. She was learning from a 14-year old how to be okay with who she was. She was standing taller and speaking up more because that's would Lucy would do. But what Sabrina wished more than anything, for herself and every girl in the world, was that she learned it earlier.

The good news was Sabrina was beginning to get it, trust herself more, and soon she began to realize she didn't make bad choices in love, she just never believed she could make good ones, or trust her instincts. But that was changing, she could feel it. No more distrust and anxiety, only love and self acceptance from now on. Forever. Swear on *High School Musical Three-SENIOR YEAR!*

Now don't forget, date with Hottie in one week and need to prepare accordingly. The Best Dress Shop Ever. Sleek, elegant dresses that Sabrina LOVED. Every year at the beach she would head into town and shop at her favorite store. But this was going to have to be the mack daddy of all dresses. She needed to carry on this new HOTNESS and knew this was just the place to do it. And sure enough there it was. The dress. A beautiful fitted strapless black top to the waist, bright white flirty bottom with huge black flowers. Tight, short and just what the Hottie ordered. Size 6 please. Did you hear that size 6? Sabrina was determined to get rid of the "Bubble Butt" Dr. Narcissist pointed out to her on any occasion. Guess what Doc? Gone. Better than ever. Kiss my gorgeous ASS!

GASP. Twirl, one more twirl. STUNNING. Fits perfectly and off sets her dark hair and bright eyes. Perfect. Ready, Set, HOT.

Sylvia

After a week of the steamiest text messages you have ever read, sun, and fun, Sabrina was ready to come home. Tan, relaxed and rested she walked into her apartment and breathed in the smell of Vanilla Musk, oh, and by the way, this is only $12 dollars at Tar-geaah, Fragrance section. Humming Bird on the bottle, pass it on.

The night Sabrina returned from the beach she was having dinner with Preppy and Lyssie, her neighbors and close friends. They were introducing her to "a friend" that they desperately wanted Sabrina to meet. As she got ready her thoughts were on Hottie. She knew she should keep dating and stay on the market but the truth was while the attention was fun, it was really exhausting. Sabrina just wanted to cut the shit and meet someone great to love like crazy. And not crazy in the sick, addicted, have to be with you way, crazy in the I get you, you get me, unspoken bond that unites hearts. Simple, right?

> Dear God,
>
> Sabrina Davis here. Where is he??????? I am so tired!!!!! And I swear on the Bible if you respond, be patient, I am not sure I will call again.
>
> Love, Sabrina

Good old God. What she could say about this friendship that had been with her from childhood? She can remember as far back as four years old laying in her, guess what color…PINK canopy bed talking to God about her day, her dreams, (which may have been for a new Barbie that didn't have polio) and asking Him to love and protect her family. God was always there. An anchor in her heart that never left her. When she was pissed, she told Him, happy, He knew, sad the tears sent the message and searching, The answers always came. No booming voice from heaven answers, just the guidance and love you need through people and places that get you where you need to go.

He was, besides Kat of course, her best friend. And she could tell Him anything. ANYTHING. Even when she was sure she about to sin (aka have a torrid night of passionate, premarital, raunchy sex). Over the years this friendship had become so real and true that there was nothing she wouldn't say. And maybe that's what was so important to her. She could be totally real and He didn't care. He just loved her, without conditions or judgment. Whether Sabrina was mean or kind, stingy or giving, happy or sad, God was there. And that is exactly what she wanted with the man, maybe even Hottie, of her dreams.

So off to dinner with Preppy and Lyssie to, yet again, have an introduction to someone her friends were convinced she would LOVE. "The Guy" was charming, very funny, in that one-liner dead pan face kind of way, and handsome for sure. But no spark. No inside, what Sabrina's father refers to as, "SIZZLE."

This was his big thing, Sabrina's Dad, or Sylvia as she affectionately referred to him, because he was so clearly a Jewish mother in his past life. SOOOOOO WHO IS HE, WHAT DOES HE DOOOOOO is there any Sizzzzzzzzzzzzzzzzle?

Like every good Jewish mother does, Sylvia, not wanting his Sabrina to be without love for one more minute, did what comes naturally to all Jewish mothers, he set her up on a blind date. When Sabrina probed Sylvia for details, all she got was the typical Jewish mother response. "He is a great guy, with a great job, who lives in a great house."

"Great," thought Sabrina, "how greatly boring." But like all good Jewish daughters do, Sabrina was not willing to disappoint her darling Sylvia. So with a "great" dress Sabrina set out to meet "The Great Guy."

The Great Guy had proposed an evening at The Ballet, and Sabrina accepted, because after all, Sabrina Davis was a very mature, wise, cultured, patron-of-the-arts kind of girl. Sabrina and The Great Guy are seated and ready for what Great Guy assured her would be a "Great Ballet." Curtain opens, and ten men, dressed in tights, charge the stage and begin doing "Great" formations in which they hold hands, twirl around, and skip across the stage in perfect unison.

Sabrina feels her shoulders start to shake, eyes water, and no, Oh please, God, no, she feels a snort about to form as she is in absolute hysterics over men in tights leaping across the stage. And now she cannot compose herself, and while the ever so appreciative patron-of-the-arts crowd is taking it all in, about to Bravo for these very talented men who can pliate' so well, Sabrina, is hunched over in her seat, nostrils flaring, (this happens to her when she gets laughing too hard, family trait) face contorted in an all out GA-FAAW-WWW laugh. And just when she gets it together the ballerina men join hands and leap into the air, and in perfect synchronicity FLUTTER their toes. This is what does Sabrina in. She is now in a full on snort fest.

"Great Guy" leans over, "You okay??"

"Oh, of course," Sabrina tries to say very patron-of-the-arts seriously. And with that she excuses herself to make a beeline for the rest room where she can GAFAWWW in peace. As she literally climbs over the very serious art patrons to get to the exit, she finds herself running to the bathroom tears streaming down her face, nostrils flaring, unable to gain her composure.

Stall locked. Sabrina speed dials her two older sisters to three-way call, because she knows her sisters, more than anyone on the earth, will totally get why she is in hysterics.

Belle: Hi! (Silence on the other end.) Hello????

Tess: Sabrina, Hello, are you there????

Sabrina: (Engulfed in laughter, silent on the other end, hysterical, nostrils in a full on flare cannot even speak.)

Belle: SABRINA??? Helloooo? Are You there???

Tess: Belle, what is going on? Sabrina, are you THERE???

Sabrina: It's, it's (Snort. Gasp. Wheeze.) OMG. It's…(more silence, wheeze …ballet...men in tights, and I can see their…(silence, wheeze, more silence)...Ba…Ba...BALLS! Men in Tights with (Gafawww laughter), BAWLS! !

Belle and Tess's simultaneous response: Silence, wheeze, gasp, snort, their nostrils flaring. (Thank you Grandfather for passing this on to the next generation.) More silence. Cackle. High pitched Cackle, with a hint of a snort and a gasp for air. More wheezing. "Ba-ba-BAWLS-Ah HAAAAAAAAAAAA."

The three of them are unable to even speak, and in the silence of gasping, wheezing and snorting Sabrina feels grateful that Belle and Tess, her ever loyal and true big sisters will always be there to share in a good old snort, nostril flaring, belly ache laugh. THANK GOD FOR SISTERS, pass it on.

And as the Great Evening comes to end, Sabrina very politely and patron-of-the-arts seriously says to her date, "Thank you, I had a GREAT time."

And till this day, Sylvia stills asks with confusion and concern, as every Jewish mother does, "Soooooooo, whatever happened to the Great Guy…."

But let's get back to the Sizzle. The jaw dropping stomach-flip-flopping sizzle. Sabrina, no matter how hard she wanted to deny it, knew Sylvia was dead on. There had to be stomach dropping sizzle. Spark. Fire.

Over the last few years, Sabrina decided to date more "practically" instead of basing first impression on attraction. The reality was, however, that even though she had pretended it wasn't important, she only came to the conclusion that sizzle is the glue that sticks from day one. Sabrina had had enough "practical" dates (aka financially stable, emotionally mature, nice guys, who you have no

physical attraction to) to know that dating without sizzle is like putting bamboo shoots in your finger nails for fun.   No sizzle? No
way. NEXT! No more settling for anything less than that. Damn it,
Sabrina thought Sylvia was always right.

SAHOTTIE.

Date night is here. Sabrina spends the day sunning on her terrace and removing any and all, remotely embarrassing, items from her bathroom. As she got ready she felt strangely peaceful and excited all at the same time. Usually before a date, she would be obsessing about the way she looked and analyzing with Kat for hours about what to wear, say, do, etc. etc. By this time, her bedroom would be filled with clothes and Kat would try to talk her off the ledge of sheer anxiety. But not this time, no analyzing, no obsessing, just peace. This was really weird. Who was Hottie and why was he having this effect on her?

Sabrina opens the door and there before her eyes stands Hottie Fratatti looking adorable. Like, SO ADORABLE. Bright eyed, huge grin on his face and pressed blue and white oxford that shows his fabulously long, gorgeously sculpted torso. When he lays eyes on Sabrina, he is SPEECHLESS. Like I am so overwhelmed by your beauty I can't breathe and will never recover from the sight of you, Sabrina "Darling" Davis.

> Dear God,
>   Please let Hottie pass out right here so I can take a picture of this and know that I literally made a man fall to his knees and pass out cold.
> Love, Sabrina

Okay, a girl can dream right?

"WOW" he says. "WOW back!" she says. And boom, it's as if they have known each other FOREVER. They are talking non-stop about their weeks, hands slightly touching, and they are like two old friends. Except these two old friends want to jump each other and get totally naked, effective immediately. Don't worry, they didn't! Sabrina was too hungry, and they were going to one of her favorite restaurants, SHINE. A romantic little place that had the best duck you have ever had in your life. Sabrina loved duck, the crispier the better, and as long as she didn't start quacking, she was going to keep eating duck.

As they strolled arm and arm towards SHINE, Sabrina could not stop smiling. She loved that Hottie was interesting and outgoing and just comfortable in his own skin. Maybe that's what it was. Hottie liked himself and was secure in that. He had his very own pizzazz and zest for life, no need to mooch off of hers. Sabrina referred to the pizzazz moochers as ENERGY DRAINERS, and she had dated enough of them to be able to spot them immediately.

These are the men who lack self esteem and pizzazz of their own. They are attracted to you for all the right reasons. You are charming, beautiful, intelligent and live life with gusto. THEY LOVE IT. This is what they have been searching for, and you my dear are the ONE, the one they are going to try and rob!

They come on strong, engaging and charming and will very subtly begin to grab hold of your enthusiasm, passion for life and creative energy. They will take it on and ride on your coat tails constantly looking at you with puppy-dog eyes asking, more like begging for your security, strength and joie de vivre. Sabrina had spent enough time with this type that she knew while they looked grown up on the outside, on the inside they were screaming babies longing for attention, security, pizzazz, and sparkle of their own.

Here's how Sabrina had come to realize she was in the presence of an energy drainer, she would feel exhausted, anxious, weird and like some other alien form had abducted her and taken her to the mother ship for an experiment. She had become an expert at detecting this and the minute she saw the writing on the wall she would RUN, do not pass go, do not collect 200 dollars, RUN FORREST RUN.

Here's the truth Sabrina learned from the energy drainers, you simply can't give someone else your passion and zest for life, it is something you either have for yourself or don't. True love is in the best of ways, supposed to enhance your life in a positive, creative way. Anytime you are drained, weary, confused and anxious, you can be sure, you were dating an energy drainer. Luckily, by the grace of God, Sabrina had been spared from these poor slobs and always got out fast enough to keep her pizzazz in tact.

Now here's the thing with Hottie, he was just as enthusiastic and pizazzy as Sabrina. Now granted, while it was way too early to give Hottie this much credit, she secretly hoped her blink was right. Hottie seemed to be comfortable in who he was and simply out to enjoy a good time. No agenda, no trying to prove anything or make him fall for her, although she was dammit.

As they approached Shine, Hottie rushed ahead and opened the door for her (mental note, good manners). Brace yourselves, because this my dear friends is Sabrina's most favorite part. As they walked into SHINE, ALL eyes fell upon them. Sabrina even heard a fork fall. Oh Shit, Sabrina thought, spinach in my teeth for sure. Or, maybe worse, lipstick on my teeth. Or maybe THE worst, I have a big pimple that just made its way to the surface and everyone can see it. Nope, guess again! It was them! SA-HOTTIE (Sabrina and Hottie combined) had made their debut and people were stunned! Like staring stunned. Hottie leans in, "Why is everyone staring at us?"

Dear God,

Sabrina Davis here. Were you really listening to me when years ago I told you how completely shallow I am and long to have true love so big that everyone in the room sees it, knows it, feels it and is stunned by it? And that oh by the way, we would be devastatingly gorgeous together?

Love, Sabrina

Dear Sabrina,

God here. Of course I was listening. How could
I not, You NEVER stop talking.

Love, God

Right, she would have to work on that. Thank God.

So, there they were all eyes upon them, enjoying the most romantic dinner EVER. And here's the thing, Sabrina ate, A LOT,
talked, laughed, listened, and locked lips with this Hottie all through
dinner. She was one hundred percent herself, duck and all (although
it was not nearly crispy enough).

After dinner, they headed to The Pearl, an old hotel in town
known for its Shakespearian Mid-Summer Nights Dream courtyard.
They sipped champagne and snuggled up close just enjoying the
summer evening air. Hottie entertained her with hysterical stories
of a childhood riddled with husky jeans and acne. Damn that Hottie,
he was so freakin cute. Even the thought of him in huskies with zits
was adorable.

Now you are probably dying to know what happened at the
end of the night. But here is the thing, even Sabrina knew that this
thing between them was so sacred, so special, so different, that not
even she wanted to share the details. She wanted to keep it right
inside her heart to cherish and honor.

But, here are a few hints: OMG the best EVER most electrifying, sweet, earth moving, heart melting, soul touching, insanely
passionate, intimate life-changing experience of her life. And those
are all the details you get.

Big Girls Don't Cry

Hottie hugged her hard and told Sabrina he was going to The City next week for business. He wanted her to join him for a few days and stay at The Hotel where they would have romantic dinners and take in the sites. The fact was Sabrina wanted to go anywhere and everywhere with this man. If he had asked her to go Mexico for the month, she would have. Thank God, she renewed her passport. Sabrina said she would think about it, and they, planned to talk in a few days. Kiss Kiss Hug Hug. Grope Grope. Door shuts.

And this is where sheer anxiety sets in. Sabrina feels her heart start to race and now she is in full on, riddled with anxiety, sweaty palms, panic mode. Sabrina is suddenly very aware that this is all very GRAY, and did she mention this is so not a color she is fond of?

Dear God,

Sabrina Davis here. This is a tricky one please advise.

Love, Sabrina

Over dinner, they had discussed Hottie's separation. It was the script Sabrina had heard over and over again in her office counseling hundreds of couples.

Get Married. Have Kids. Work. Work. Busy. Kids. Work. Busier. Stress. Strangers. Time of death: about 10-15 years depending on the couple. This was the story every couple who walked into Sabrina's office had. Sitting in wing chairs staring at her waiting for Sabrina to save their marriage. And guess what, deep down this made Sabrina angry. Very angry. She thought people had become lazy, shockingly lazy, about love.

Willing to postpone, put off, too busy, the kids, the bills, the this, the that. Love can wait. And maybe it was because Sabrina had never had this Love that made her angry. She knew deep down in her heart that when Love came to stay she would do anything and everything to keep it, nourish it, grow it and protect it. She didn't want the obligatory peck goodbye have a good day honey. She wanted a smack on the ass, you're the best thing around, I LOVE YOU, Sabrina Davis, goodbye. But so many had lost it. And so many were content to let it be lost. It seemed people were putting off love thinking they would get to it when they had time. ?????

This was so bizarre to Sabrina. Ohhhh Sabrina, You naïve, never married, never having children, or an annoying pain in the ass husband, or house, or full time job, and house to take care of. Oh Darling Sabrina, WAKE UP! You just don't get it!

But she was awake. Wide awake taking it all in. Every detail of why loved worked and why it didn't. You see, Sabrina had been obsessed with love since day one. Even as a child, she knew Barbie and Ken had to sit down in their dream house at the end of a long day and connect. Now granted, their was probably a maid and skip-per had not yet come onto the scene, but she KNEW THIS. You HAVE to make time to connect with LOVE. The ones you love, the things you love, the places you love.

Sabrina had always known from childhood that she wanted a job where she could help people connect and celebrate this love in every way. She wanted to teach people how to honor, love, and have relationships that were so deep, true, real, mind-blowing pure LOVE. If anyone asked her what she wanted to be when she grew up, this was the answer: Help people or be an actress. And guess what, she was a little bit of both.

As a therapist you help people, but you also have to act like you know what you are doing. And even when Sabrina wasn't so sure what to do, she would fall into the rhythm of relying on the wisdom and love of her faithful friend God and trust that she would know eventually. But the key was to never join the anxiety or drama of the client. Simply be an accepting loving presence willing to sit with them in the pain and sort it out step by step. Even if on the inside you wanted to sob with them, hug them, tell them it was all going to work out and you too had survived a heart-wrenching experience. This was the acting part.

Sometimes after a client left, the stories she heard would bring her to her knees in tears. But this she knew was the beauty of her job. Feeling. Feeling all the love, pain, sorrow, doubt, shame, guilt, fear. Feeling it with them while holding a strong steady presence of peace. She LOVED her job and more than that she LOVED people. And Sabrina knew that she had to take all this love and use it for good. So, after studying love incessantly, she had to come to realize there were some great examples out there of couples who got it right. Let's start with her favorite one.

Exhibit A.

Ronald and Nancy Regan. Political parties aside please. Look at the pictures, read the quotes. Ronny had a pretty high-stress job. Lots of pressure on him. But in every picture, you see they are connected, touching in some way, looking at each other adoringly. Take a look at Ronny's love letters to Nancy. They cherished one another and despite the stress of the cold war and nuclear attack, they honored LOVE and were not willing for one minute to let it go. They got it.

Exhibit B.

Paul Newman and Joanne Woodward. Beautiful, charming Hollywood stars who despite living in tinsel town, built a beautiful family and a huge charitable organization helping children with chronic illnesses. They had their priorities straight and stayed true to what mattered most, their family. They definitely got it.

Last one, Exhibit C.

Gene Simmons and Shannon Tweed. Okay fine, Sabrina will admit it: I, Sabrina Davis am somewhat addicted to reality TV and secretly would not dare miss a new episode of Gene Simmons Family Jewels. Now, it's not the content of the episodes that kept Sabrina watching. It was the love and respect Sabrina saw between Gene and Shannon that intrigued her and kept her attention. Here's what they had FUN! Laughter! Sillyness! Sure life gets serious and stressful but these two laugh all the time.

All too often, Sabrina had watched couples stop laughing. No laughter, no fun, we must be focused on the children and finances and be on schedule at all times because we have someplace to be. And Sabrina thought, where is everyone trying to get to?? What about taking a break and doing what Gene and Shannon do: LAUGH. Big belly aching, silly nonsense laughter. Yup, Gene + Shannon=totally get it. (Gene, please propose to Shannon, I think your wedding would be a hoot.)

So, Sabrina took all this observation and came up with her own personal love mission statement.

I, Sabrina Davis, swear on Jonathan and Jennifer Hart, her most favorite couple, vow to honor love, when it eventually (please God hurry up!) comes my way. When True Love walks in, I will love him madly. I will make time for him and let him know that I WANT him, NEED him, but not in the sick, can't live without you, insecure need, more, need you in my life because you are just so damn cool to hang out with. She would look right into his eyes, every day, and let him know that LOVE was here. And she would touch him, so many clients complained to her about this. No affection, no tenderness, no touch. Nope, she would grope the hell out of him. Because this is what she knew: Love is a gift. A precious gift that we can only hope to receive. And when you get it, do not, under any circumstances take it for granted. NEVER EVER.

And this my friends is why she had to let Hottie go. Gasp! What??? Yup. It's true. Hottie was in the stage of having lost love. Marriage over, or about to be. Done. Game over. Sabrina had counseled many through this phase and it's one of the most painful, awful, heart wrenching experiences to witness. People who are in this phase start to wake up. Sabrina has seen it for herself. They begin to slow down and take a good hard look at why love was lost and how it had died. And this is where they start to grow. The pain and regret and overwhelming guilt pushes people to a higher more enlightened phase. As they wake up, they start to reprioritize, make healthy changes, and most vow, never ever again to be careless with love.

This is where Hottie was. He was at the very beginning of the awakening path and here was Sabrina, smack damn in front of him, blinding him with her overwhelming beauty and charming personality (or so she thought). Sabrina knew, in her heart and genius therapist mind that if she stuck around she was going to seriously thwart Hottie's growth and ability to make the changes he needed to figure out why love was lost. How very mature of her to come to this conclusion right?

Dear God,
This sucks
Love, Sabrina

Dear Sabrina,
I know. But know this. I LOVE YOU.
Love, God

Oh Great. Put the pressure on. Put the Almighty, I am God, do the Right thing pressure on. Decision made. Call Hottie first thing in the morning and say goodbye. She was for sure, going to make this call from her office. Somehow the four walls and degrees hanging would give her the "I am a genius therapist who knows what to do in every situation and this is the absolute right most mature and very professional thing to do."

But in her heart this is what she was thinking. I am a girl who met the most unbelievable guy and I am falling fast and hard and think everything about him is adorable and wonderful, and HE GETS ME, and I have to let him go. And this is heartbreaking. So Sabrina does the Marsha Brady "I hate my life" throws herself down on the floor of her office and cries. Big Hard Ugly cry. In case you don't know what the ugly cry is, it's when your face contorts into Tourette's like twitches, you turn bright red with a hint of purple and you sort of gasp for air making strange sounds that sound like the whining of a hurricane that is full on in the eye of the storm. Ugly cry. She was in full on ugly cry WHY GOD WHY mode.

Okay, Drama Queen, calm down and make the call. Deep breathe. Stare at your degree. You are very mature and professional and you can do this. Right. On it. Hottie answers on the first ring.

Hottie: Hi gorgeous. (Nooo, don't make this harder for me!!! Sabrina thinks. And she loves that he called her gorgeous.)

Sabrina: (Very serious therapist tone) Hello. Listen, I was thinking, about meeting you in the city for business. Its just, well, I umm, have a full week of clients booked and I can't really cancel last minute (Liar! Tell him! Come on Sabrina you can do this.)

Hottie: Hey, sweetie, are you okay??? (Oh great make it worse. Mr. Intuitive knows Sabrina so well he can tell she is not herself. And Sabrina is relieved on one hand that he gets her and devastated on another because she has to let him go.)

Sabrina: (Voice cracks. Eyes well. DO NOT CRY SABRINA. Breathe. Degrees dammitt. Focus.) Not really, its just I have been thinking and you and I are in such different places right now, and you are just in the beginning of this whole separation thing and I just don't feel like the timing is right for us and...(now she can't talk and is really silently sobbing about to, oh dear God no, cross over to ugly cry.)

Hottie: Listen, I totally get it. I just want you to know, I think you are the coolest chick. Attraction aside, I just really think you are awesome. (Knife in heart!) Why don't we have this talk in person when I get back into town.?

Oh great idea Hottie, then I can stare at you and think of nothing but wanting to kiss you and won't have my secret degree powers, and I will not be able to do this. Really, stellar idea. That Hottie, so damn smart.

Sabrina: Perfect. Sounds good see you when you get back. Click. Sabrina!!!!

> Dear God,
>
> I am a horrible person. Please don't send me to hell immediately. Please understand that I want to do the right thing but think Hottie has special powers that make me weak in the knees. Please help me. Give me courage and strength and Ohhhhhhhhh GAWD THIS IS HORRIBLE!!!!!!!!!!!!!!!!!
>
> Love, Sabrina

> Dear Sabrina,
>
> Calm down. I am always here.
>
> Love, God

And this is when Sabrina felt like a huge hypocrite. How many times had she sat in her office with women who were smitten with men who were getting divorced and pursuing them hard core? Sabrina would always say the same thing, "not available yet, wait till its done, this could be messy."

Now here Sabrina was, smack dab in the same scenario and she suddenly felt hypocritical. Perhaps love isn't that black and white, and while Sabrina knew she should run and not look back, she felt weak in the knees. She finally understood it, while it's easy to stand on the sidelines and shout out orders, when you're in the game, all bets are off.

CALM DOWN. CALM DOWN. Sabrina hears the voice of her best friend, God whispering in her heart. Sabrina was not comforted by these words. Calm down, right God, easy for you to say. You're not in LOVE. Gasp, what????? Easy girl. Don't go there. Back up. Yup. It was on its way she could feel it make its way toward her heart. She was really screwed. And with that Sabrina prepared for the GOODBYE FOREVER HOTTIE talk.

The Best Jeweler Ever Saves the Day

Sabrina opens the door and there is gorgeous Hottie with a small bag that is from her most favorite jeweler in the world, "The Best Jeweler Ever." Oh NOOOOOOO! Jewelry! This is off to a horrible start, Sabrina thinks to herself.

Adorable Hottie gives Sabrina a hug. The kind that screams "my darling Sabrina I missed you and never want to let you go. I'm yours forever." And the tears well up again! Sabrina, cry baby, you have got to get a hold of yourself!

> Dear God,
>> He has jewelry. SOS!
> Love, Sabrina

And as they stare at each other all googly eyed Sabrina opens the package and GASP!!!! A beautiful silver turquoise bracelet with diamonds. OMG OMG, she had the bracelet spotted months ago and drooled over it, and here it was on her wrist from Hottie! How did he know?????

Tears well up. Sabrina, you have to be PMSing or something because this is really ridiculous.

"How did you know?" Sabrina says.

"Know what?" replies Hottie. "I just picked the one that looked like you."

OMG! He even knows her taste without knowing. And this is when she wants to scream from her terrace to the sun, the moon, the stars and anyone listening…"HE GETS ME KNOWS WHAT I LIKE ADORES ME AND I LOVE HIM." Well, she thinks so any-way. Hottie begins the talk.

Hottie: Look, I never ever expected this. To meet you. To feel this way. (Please define "This," this love, this attraction, what is "this?" Sabrina thinks to herself.)

Hottie continues: This strongly. (Okay, girls we all know this is code for falling in love. Yippee!) And I know that you and I are in totally different places right now (translation: you are free and clear and I have lots of baggage), but I don't want to let "this" (there it is again) go. I can't Sabrina. I don't want to, not for a minute let this go. I have to see what "this" (please just say it! This unbelievable feeling of LOVE! and he sort of says it.) This feeling that is so strong and right. It's like a pull and force much bigger than anything I have ever experienced (read again, EVER! Never in his life!!! WAHOOOOOOOO)."

Attention World: Hottie Fratatti has never ever felt a feeling like he has for the one, the only Sabrina "Darling" Davis. Applause. Cheers. Thank you World!! He likes me, he really really likes (maybe even LOVES) me!

"And really Sabrina, what I need to know is how you feel. Do you feel what I feel?"

And he takes her hands and is staring deeply into her eyes. Practically putting her into a trance with those eyes. And Sabrina is total jello, and is now blinded completely by the glow of her new diamond turquoise silver shiny bracelet.

"I feel the exact same way, Hottie."

He hugs her, and kisses her gently on the, brace yourself girls, FOREHEAD. The forehead kiss. Sabrina's favorite. The forehead kiss that represents protection, tenderness, sweetness, and innocence. And it's hers. Right now. Hottie's lips on her forehead. Putty in his hands. Done.

As he holds her hands he begins to laugh. Like hysterical cannot breathe hunched over gasping for air laugh. And Sabrina is totally confused. "What is so funny?" Now he can barely speak.

"Your, HAAAAA, your, H-A-N-D-S!"

And now Sabrina is laughing because the sight of her adorable

Hottie in hysterics is hilarious. What? What about my hands?"

Now he is laughing so hard he is grabbing his stomach. And he spits it out, "They are so weird!!! And creepy, like spider web fingers!!!" And now he is practically on the ground in hysterical fits of laughter.

Okay here it is. Sabrina's hands. People have either two responses to her hands and here they are:

You have the most adorable little tiny baby hands and nails how cute. (This was the one her mother went with.)
OR
You have the most fucked up wrinkly tiny hands I have ever seen. What the hell happened?

Refer to Euro. London guy she dated very briefly almost a year ago. In perfect British totally condescending snotty accent, "Do you spend much time in the sun?" Translation: Your hands are really wrinkly and strange and suggest toxic amounts of sun which can only lead me to the conclusion, Mr. I am so worldly because I am British, you Sabrina Davis are a Sun-a-holic.

Go to bloody hell, you ignorant wanker. I had a rare disease as a kid that required massive amounts of steroids and I think the side effect was wrinkly baby hands. Nope, Sabrina couldn't say it. Instead, she stuffed her hands in her pocket and felt that old familiar shame creep on in. She was ashamed of her hands and wanted new ones. ASAP.

So here's the weird thing. Hottie is in hysterics over her hands, and Sabrina doesn't care. No Shame, no stuffing her hands into her pockets, no embarrassment. She is actually laughing with him and now they are both hysterical. Sabrina is doing weird spider man-finger moves, and Hottie is laughing harder begging, no pleading with her to stop. And this is where she wants to laugh and cry at the same time.

50

This Hottie was changing her, for the better, and everything about this, EVERYTHING, is different, and true and comfortable and hysterical and sooooo right. The decision is made right then and there. Sabrina cannot let go of Hottie, not yet anyway. And he cannot let go of her. Thus SaHottie (remember, Sabrina + Hottie.) is born on a warm summer evening as the sounds of hysterical laughter fill the air and the stars and moon are shining brighter as if to confirm: This is it you two, this is what's its all about, EN-JOY!!!!!!!!!!!!!!

T.L.F.
True Love Forever

And they do. they enjoy every single minute of it. Thus begins long romantic dinners and hours of talking and laughing and kissing and dancing and hugging and more laughing and, oh well, you get it. Sahottie is in full effect, and Sabrina has to pinch herself to make sure this is not a dream.

As the summer nights make the transition into crisp cool air, Hottie suggests a weekend in the country where they can "leaf peep" and just so you know, she thinks this is the queerest expression ever. Leaf peeping. All she can think of is a creepy child molester guy darting in and out of trees "peeping" on the foliage. The expression always makes her cringe, but of course, she thinks it's adorable that Hottie uses this expression. When she gives him her take on it, once again, you guessed it, he is in hysterics. Did Sabrina mention that Hottie thinks she is the most hysterical woman he has ever (emphasis on EVER) met? Yup. You heard it here first. Sabrina Darling Davis, funniest woman ever, to Hottie. Does it get any better than this???? Yes, dear girlys, much better…..

Recap. Sahottie was going to have their first weekend away. And guess what, kryptonite was coming to. Remember, the shiny red convertible Ferrari? There she was, Sabrina Darling Davis, in a convertible driving through the twisty mountain roads of the country feeling like a movie star. A movie star who was spending the weekend with someone who was actually becoming more than a romantic interest. They were increasingly headed for best friend status.

Over the weeks, Sabrina and Hottie had fallen into a rhythm of peace and total one hundred percent comfort around one another. Sometimes they would snuggle up reading…she the latest *People*, he the *New York Daily News*, and she would stop and show him a hideous dress of the latest Hollywood couple to blow up or let him know the breaking news history. And get this girls, he would listen. He would stop, put the paper down, look at the picture and begin a full on discussion with Sabrina about the details of why the dress was so hideous or his take on the break up. Full on discussion. Can you believe it?????

It was this sort of ease and flow as to why they were becoming best friends as well as lovers. (Which is another sort of queer cheesy word, but that's the only way Sabrina could describe it.) Friends and Lovers. I know I know, cringe at the cheese factor.

Don't worry, Kat would never be replaced, but there was something so cool about having that friendship bond with the person you made out with on the regular basis. Sabrina was sure she had never experienced this friendship thing, and she really liked it. A LOT (say like Jim Carrey in *Dumb and Dumber*, ALOTTTT.) Okay, back to country get away.

They arrive at "The Most Romantic Inn Ever," and as they pull into the quaint country town, Sabrina points out an old country playhouse that she and her family would visit every summer to watch plays. And as she describes in detail that this was where she became inspired to be an actress at the age of eight years old, Hottie pulls kryptonite over and insists they go in for a look.

Hand in hand, they walk into the playhouse, and Sabrina is overwhelmed with the smell of cedar and the musky summer air. She can see the excitement and anticipation she felt as a little girl, taking in every detail of these magical summer evenings in which the stage would become alive. And as she shares with Hottie her memories and her dreams of acting on that very stage, she notices that he is locked into her eyes, taking in every detail of the conversation, picturing his darling as a little girl with bright wide eyes and big dreams in her heart. Sabrina is moved that he cares, cares about every detail of what this little playhouse meant to her. As they leave the playhouse arm and arm, Hottie squeezes her close and says "Thank you so much for sharing that with me," and Sabrina thinks that her heart will melt and she is beyond overwhelmed with love and gratitude for her precious Hottie.

Next stop is "The Very Charming Little Book Store." The kind that have tiny little nooks and crannies where you can get lost in the books for hours. And as they stroll through every nook and cranny they come across a beautiful antique globe. They sit for what seems like hours, pointing out all the places they have been and describing in detail the adventures they have had. And dear sweet Hottie is pointing out countries and cities and mispronouncing every single one, like completely butchering every one.

Here's the thing, rather than admit he can't pronounce them properly he says them really fast as if Sabrina won't know. She is in hysterics as she decides right then and there to give Hottie a tutorial on Hooked on Phonics. And as she tries to teach him the correct pronunciation, they start to laugh harder, because the truth is, she has the same problem. So the two of them are sounding out the vowels in the hopes between the two of them, they might get the pronunciation right. But guess what, NOT EVEN CLOSE. They even had the same pronunciation challenges. This was definitely true love for sure, swear on Hooked on Phonics.

As they stroll the streets of "The Most Romantic Little Country Town," Hottie insists on taking Sabrina shopping. Like can't wait wants to go and pick things out for Sabrina. GASP! A man who wants to go shopping!!!!!!!!!!!! Really God, this is too much. But notice Sabrina isn't talking to God so much these days. She is too busy with Hottie. But don't worry, God is still there, and she knows they will be talking a lot in the months to come. She can feel it.

They enter "The Designer Dress Shop" hand and hand to shop away. Sabrina and Hottie pick out all the size 6 dresses (and guess what, all this love stuff was shrinking her to an almost 4, but not quite there yet.) As she heads to the dressing room, Hottie is totally content to sit and wait. You may want to read that again. A man shopping. Sitting and waiting. No newspaper. No cell phone. Just sitting contently as the woman he loves (at least Sabrina is beginning to think, although not yet official) tries on dresses.

As she puts the first dress on she notices it's a little snug, like can't get over hips snug. Hmmm, Sabrina thinks. This is really weird, checks tag, Yup 6 for sure. So thinking it's the way the dress is cut she tries on another one. Tighter. GASP. NONE of the size 6 dresses fit her. Like not even close. Oh NOOOO, Sabrina starts to panic.

"Honey, is everything okay?" Hottie peaks in the curtain.

"Ahh, yes darling, can you grab a few sizes, ahh, mumble mumble, 8's."

And here is where you may need to sit down before reading this next part. Sabrina peaks out of the curtain, and Hottie and the sales girl that he has asked to help him (gasp, a man asking for help!!) proceed to go through every rack looking for size 8 dresses that Sabrina will like. Here's the kicker, when the saleslady picks out a few 8's and shows them to Hottie, he stops her and says, "No thank you, Sabrina will definitely not like that, its soooo not her."

Okay, I swear, Hottie is not gay, believe me, she would know by now. Nope not gay, just a man who knows what his gal likes and is not willing to make her settle for anything less than perfect. Sabrina is watching all this behind the curtain and, aw shucks, she was heading, more like hurling, toward true love status.

So, there she is in the dressing room ready for the 8's and Oh, Dear God. Same thing, tight. You have got to be kidding. I, Sabrina Davis, swear on my love of pink dresses, will not under any circumstances be forced to try on double digits. No freakin way. Not happening. She had come too far worked too hard, for this, and now, she was forced to make the decision.

Patient, Sweet, Wonderful Hottie peaks in. Sabrina whispers the problem and guess what, no shame about it. By this point, Sabrina would usually lie to the guy and tell him the dresses were not her style. But not with Hottie, nope, she let's him know they have crossed the great divide into 10's! and Hottie doesn't bat an eye and is off again (with the saleslady for help!!!!) to collect every 10 in the place.

Once again Sabrina bravely goes for the 10 and GASP! PUKE! She can't zip it!!!!!!!!!!!! And there is ever supportive Hottie trying to, with all his Hottie might and strength, zip the dress. But it won't budge. And dear Hottie does not have the heart to tell his darling Sabrina that he cannot even get the size 10 zipped.

So instead of saying a word about it, he starts laughing. Hysterically laughing. Now, Sabrina is laughing. And there they are Sahottie squeezed into the dressing room in hysterics over the whole thing. And Hottie is kissing her (on the forehead!!!) telling Sabrina that she is beautiful and not to worry he will go try for the, and he breaks into fits of laughter. He will go get the stutter, gasp for air, more laughter, the.....12's!!!!! Bahaaaaaaaa!!!!!!!!!!!!!!!!! Now they are both barely able to breathe because they are laughing so hard at the idea that Sabrina a solid 6 almost 4 cannot fit her fat ass into the size 12's. Hottie thinks this is adorable and hysterical at the same time. And Sabrina sees as she looks into his eyes in the very tiny dressing room that he has the look of true love for his big fat size 12 darling and she LOVES it.

As they walk out of the store, still giddy with laughter, Hottie pulls Sabrina close and whispers into her ear, "Oh sweetie, We (yup. You read it right, WE. They have become a WE. WEEEEE) We are never shopping at Betsy Burton again, I promise."

And with that he squeezes her close and gives her a big kiss on the yup, you guessed it, the forehead! This is the thing about true love, to which Sabrina was quite certain, she and Hottie had reached. True love will forever protect the one he loves from the shame and humiliation of shopping at Betsy Burton, or any thing else, for that matter, that would ever inflict pain on his true love. And this was what Hottie wanted to do, protect his dear Sabrina from anything hurtful. Damn that Hottie. He was making her fall fast and hard.

With that tender moment between them they began laughing hysterically all over again at the entire fashion debacle and decided to let BB know how they felt right then and there.

> Dear Betsy Burton,
>
> Please rethink your sizing. Tragic really. Potential to make women either starve for life or go on a carb binge. And I am sure you know Ms. Burton, what carb binging has the potential to do (If not please refer to the memo.) Guess what, my almost True Love agrees that your sizing is horrendous. He was very upset seeing his Darling traumatized by the experience.
>
> Forever not shopping at your store ever again, Sa-Hottie.
> (Sabrina Davis + Hottie Fratatti=TLF true love forever.)

And as the laughter continued Hottie got a delicious bottle of red wine, and they settled into watch the sunset at "The Most Romantic Inn." As they sat back in their Adirondack chairs, Sabrina was trying to take in every detail of the gorgeous sunset as splashes of pink and purple (her absolute favorite colors) danced across the sky. It was there that they began talking about their childhoods. What Sabrina and Hottie shared growing up was parents who adored them and loved them unconditionally. Sabrina wondered if this was why love and laughter came so very easily to them, they were taught it from day one.

Sabrina thought back to all the experiences she had before with the men she had dated (and clients for that matter) who were damaged from not mothers, mostly fathers, who refused to give them what they longed for, acceptance and love. Sabrina could not help but think, with her deep genius therapist mind, is this why people screw up love, because they never ever know what it's like to be unconditionally accepted, adored and loved? Perhaps that was the problem. You can't give out that kind of love without ever having it as a child. And here's the thing, she and Hottie had both had that kind of love.

Hottie recounted his first day of kindergarten where his loving parents, rather than leave their precious Hottie, parked the car right outside the kindergarten window so that if he ever felt afraid or missed them, he could look outside and see them waving and cheering him on. And Sabrina recounted her first day of kindergarten, when her entire family, parents, sisters and brother, walked her all the way to school and cheered as she walked up the steps by herself. And Sabrina, the ever child aspiring actress, turned around and blew kisses as she skipped into the building. Perhaps it is this formative love and support that determines your success with love as an adult.

Sabrina felt sad for those who didn't have that love, rather, they had to fumble around in the uncertainty, hoping someone would love and accept them the way their parents, and again, in Sabrina's experience, mostly fathers, were never able to. And what she noticed is that even when these unloved souls got love, they ultimately rejected it, because while it felt good for a moment, they had no idea how to receive it, let alone give it back. They were forever lost in the get love reject-love-cycle. Sabrina came to the conclusion as the sun was setting and the last of the wine was poured, she and Hottie could love each other truly, madly, deeply because that's all they knew. Thank God for loving parents…pass it on.

That evening Sabrina was getting ready for dinner at The Most Romantic Restaurant which was located in The Most Romantic Inn.

As she stood in front of the mirror carefully applying her make up, she stopped and stared at her reflection. She looked gorgeous. And I don't mean because of her make up or what she was wearing. It was, no mistaking, the look of love. Her eyes were glowing, her cheeks rosy, lips full, skin radiant…yup, no question this was the glow that could only come from a girl in love. No amount of blush, foundation, or pink frosted lipstick could even come close to the utter beauty that the true love creates. Sabrina smiled taking it all in.

Tonight she was wearing the outfit that she wore the night she met Hottie. He had affectionately referred to the scarf she had worn as a shirt that night as "The Scarf," and he had often told her that it was that scarf that did him in completely that night. So tonight, she was wearing The Scarf to honor their beginning. As she opened the bathroom door and walked out into the room, Hottie was, for the second time in the history of Sahottie, SPEECHLESS. In fact, it took him a minute to even get the words out, and when he did it was more like a whisper… "You are…(pause)…unbelievably gorgeous."

And instead of saying thank you, Sabrina said "I know…," Because she did know. She knew it way down deep that this love inside her heart was the best beauty secret ever around. Here is what Hottie didn't know. Hottie didn't know that she too was utterly speechless. There he was in a dark black button down shirt that made his deep brown eyes pop. I mean she could get lost in those eyes for a long, long time. He had fitted jeans and a dark blazer and Sabrina, never ever in her entire 33 years on earth, had thought a man so unbelievably handsome. And she let him know it too, right then and there.

As they walked into The Most Romantic Restaurant hand and hand, it happened again. All eyes on them, utter silence as people's heads literally turned to watch them walk through the room. Sabrina and Hottie shared a knowing glance acknowledging that the whole room knew and felt what they already knew, they were in love. They were radiant and when you see a couple in love, you cannot help but stare, because its so damn jaw dropping gorgeous. Sahottie=jaw dropping gorgeous. Imagine that, and please pass on.

As Sabrina ate her perfectly crispy duck, she found herself staring at Hottie. I don't mean looking, I mean, I cannot take my eyes off you, and if I do for one second, it's one second way too long. And as the waitress cleared away the plates and the last of the guests cleared the dining room, Sabrina realized that they were alone.

Just of the two of them in this cozy romantic place with a warm fire going. As the light of the fire danced across Hottie's eyes, Sabrina very slowly got up from her seat, walked to his chair, put her arms around him and sat down on Hottie's lap. And very gently she took his face in her hands and began to softly kiss his face, first his eyes, then his nose, cheeks, neck…and Hottie wrapped his arms around her and held her oh so very close, buried his head in her long dark hair and gently whispered, "Sabrina Davis, I love you."

She whispered back, "Hottie Fratatti, I love you too."

No fireworks, no parade down Main Street announcing their love. No dramatic analysis of when exactly did you know and how long have you felt this way. Just this quiet tender moment that Sabrina wanted to last forever and remember every bit of. She and Hottie were officially in love…pass it on.

SCATTAMOOSH

While all girls want this type of moment to last forever, eventually you have to check out of The Most Romantic Inn ever and show up at work. And as the weeks rolled on, Sabrina realized she had not seen Kat in what seemed like forever. So she put in a call, and the plans were set. They would go to PINK and belt out karaoke all night.

You see, Sabrina LOVED karaoke, remember how she wanted to be an actress? This is how she would sow those acting oats. And she took her singing very seriously by the way. So they were off to PINK when Hottie called to say he too was on his way to PINK with some friends, and what fun, they could all sing karaoke together. Sabrina was thrilled, singing her heart out with the Hottie she loved, and the best friend she adored. What could be better??

"Bohemian Rhapsody Next!" the DJ calls out, "Next!"

"OMG," Sabrina squeezes Hottie's hand. "It's me."

"Good luck DARLING!" Hottie laughs. And there is Miss Sabrina Darling Davis microphone in hand very seriously singing Bohemian Rhapsody. "SCATTA MOOSH SCATTA MOOSH CAN YOU DO THE FANDAYGO THUNDER BOLT OF LIGHTNING…and as she is concentrating on hitting every note perfectly and taking this very seriously, because, after all, she is an aspiring actress, she glances up to see Hottie and Kat in hysterics.

They are actually holding each other up as they grab their stomachs in unison. Sabrina starts laughing too. They begin to cheer. Hottie is all smiles giving her the thumbs up, and Kat is practically drooling she is laughing so hard. Then, out of nowhere, this big Neandrethal looking girl, but could pass for a guy, hip checks Sabrina, grabs the microphone and pushes, Sabrina Darling Davis, out of the way. Her jaw drops in complete shock. Now Hottie and

Kat are laughing harder, like you just got kicked off the microphone and you are too much, and we love you, but you are so bad at karaoke that you actually got kicked off the microphone, by a big fat mean girl who may even be a boy. Gufawww.

Tears are now streaming down Hottie's face, and it's not because he is overwhelmed with deep love for his Darling. Its like this is the funniest thing he as ever seen in his life, and he is not sure he will ever be able to stop laughing or crying about this. Neither of them can speak they are laughing so hard. Kat now has her hand up in protest, as if Sabrina comes any closer to them, they will fall to the floor and die of too much laughter. Hottie is now totally leaning on Kat unable to stand he is laughing so hard.

But Sabrina does not think this is funny. Not at all in fact. And as she regains her composure having just been kicked off the karaoke stage, anger begins to rise, and she begins to consider jumping big fat microphone stealing, fun wrecker, spirit crusher girl, maybe boy, and starting an all out karaoke war. Just as she is about to stage a come back to retrieve the microphone, big strong Hottie sees his darling is hurting and right then and there he scoops Sabrina up, spins her around and says, "Lovey (this was his new one, LOVEY. How freakin adorable is that?) Lovey, don't you worry, I will buy you a karaoke bar, and you can sing your heart out every night, I promise."

Sabrina is in heaven. Her True Love rather than see her disappointed is going to buy her a karaoke bar where she can Scattamoosh all night long. Awwwww. Kat hears all this and is rolling her eyes about to throw up, but Sabrina doesn't notice, she's too busy thinking about Scattamooshing at her karaoke bar.

As they recover from the drama of Bohemian Rhapsody, it's Hottie's turn to sing. He decides on Sinatra's *New York, New York*. And much to Sabrina's surprise, Hottie is very talented, and actually a damn good singer, like every eye glued upon him good. The whole room, get this, begins cheering him on.

Sabrina and Kat's jaws are totally on the ground. Kat leans in to Sabrina without moving her gaze off of Hottie, "He's really really good."

Sabrina leans back, "I know, right?"

Sabrina loves it, all eyes on her Hottie as he literally takes the entire bar over. And now he has gone over the edge, for the grand finale he begins shouting, "God Bless America, God Bless the Troops, God Bless the USA…" (Who knew Hottie was so patriotic?) And now the place is going nuts, like cheering, people hugging and singing along nuts, and a group of Army guys are rushing the stage high fiving Hottie and begin smacking his ass. (Side note: Why do guys do this when they get over excited? What is this about?) Even Sabrina, the genius therapist, could not explain this disgusting but smacking behavior that all males seem to engage in. (IF you know the answer, please get in touch). Back to Her Hottie the star…so there he is getting his ass spanked by the Army boys, and Sabrina and Kat are taking all this in in absolute awe.

Kat leans in, gazed still locked on Hottie, "You are totally dating yourself, you know that right? You and Hottie are the same exact person!"

Sabrina leans in back without taking her eyes off Hottie, "I know, we are the exact same person…," and with that she runs and jumps on Hottie and once again he twirls her around and she screams, "YOU WERE FABULOUS!" Here they are twirling and laughing, singing and in love. It is the best most delicious feeling ever, and Sabrina never wants it to end. EVER.

The Lipstick Nazi

A few weeks later, Hottie surprises Sabrina with a weekend to The City, where they will stay at The Fancy Schmancy Hotel and take in the sights. Sabrina is thrilled because it just so happens that her brother, Cosgrove, and his adorable girlfriend, Chloe, live there, and Sabrina makes arrangements for them to all meet up and have drinks at The Fancy Schmancy Hotel. Drinks poured, introductions made, conversation flowing, and Chloe grabs Sabrina's hand and says, "Come on, bathroom, NOW."

As we all know, this is where the analysis of Hottie Fratatti will take place, and she and Chloe will squeal with excitement over the fact that Sahottie is in love and fabulous. As they get inside the Fancy Schmancy bathroom, Chloe very seriously and sternly says to Sabrina, "Open it."

Sabrina, suddenly very afraid, stammers, "What? What are you talking about???"

"You know exactly what I am talking about. We've been over this."

And Sabrina knows, she knows exactly what Chloe is referring to, she is about to get interrogated by the LIPSTICK NAZI (aka, adorable Chloe, who by the way is not at all adorable at this moment).

Sabrina hands over the purse wondering if she should ask for bread (gluten free of course, refer to carb memo) and water just in case Chloe decides to lock her up for life. Chloe fumbles around, and Sabrina prays she hid her secret weapon well. No chance. "Ahhhhh GASP. Nooooooo," Chloe says in a very not adorable voice.

Sabrina stutters, "Noo, it's not what you think, I, I."

Chloe: Wet and Wild Ultimate Pink Frost???? Wet and Wild????????????? (Sabrina tries to hide in a stall. Except it's a

Fancy Schmancy bathroom so she heads for the door.)

Chloe: Sabrina, I am officially confiscating your ultimate pink frost. You are banned from this forever. And, just in case you don't think I noticed, you are wearing it right now and it looks HIDEOUS. (Sabrina quickly licks her lips removing the evidence as quickly as possible, secretly hoping that the ultimate in the frost will disappear immediately.)

Sabrina: Okay fine, I admit it. I had a relapse!

Chloe: I was going to wait until Christmas but YOU have given me no other choice. (She says in utter disgust as she rifles through her purse.) Here.

Sabrina timidly takes the gloss and examines the label "The Best Ever Lipgloss" Champagne. And secretly Sabrina wants to scream "NOOOOOO I can't do it, I, Sabrina Davis, am addicted, like need a support group, ADDICTED to ULTIMATE PINK FROST." But Sabrina knows better. If she makes this confession to the not so adorable Lipstick Nazi, she will be forever chained to Champagne or some other dreadful neutral gloss. So, instead, she willingly takes the gloss and applies it.

"OH THANK GOD," Chloe says all too dramatically.

"Fine," says Sabrina, "but don't think I can't get more Wet and Wild. And, it's only $1.99, CHLOE!!"

Chloe stares Sabrina dead in the eyes and says, "I am ONLY doing this because I LOVE YOU."

And that my dear girls, is where the hard core lipstick intervention occurred. But at this very moment Wet and Wild Ultimate Pink Frost lives on in a secret sewn in trap door at the bottom of Sabrina's purse, so that she will never ever again have hard core evidence that she is a pink frost addict. By the way, you can purchase this glorious color at your nearest drugstore for $1.99. What girl doesn't love a bargain? Pass it on…

So here they are in The City at the Fancy Schmancy Hotel getting ready for "The Best Ever Broadway Show," and if you have not seen this show, you must! Like, immediately get there life will never ever be the same. Here's a hint…it's about a witch. So Sabrina and Hottie settle into their unbelievable, practically in the orchestra, pit seats and the show begins.

It is phenomenal, and Sabrina, once again, is wondering why on earth she has never pursued this burning desire to be an actress. She is mesmerized by the talent, music, scenery, costumes…every detail is coursing through her veins, and she is totally one hundred percent captivated. And dear sweet Hottie is captivated as well, arm around Sabrina, holding her close, deep brown eyes wide with excitement. In one scene, the main character and her true love are locked into one another's eyes, sitting face to face, arms holding one another in an embrace that forms a perfect heart, singing about how love has changed them, strengthened them, pushed them to be better, but they have to let go. At the end of the song, they let go of one another to face their fears head on, and Sabrina is practically hysterical.

Tears streaming down her face, she watches them confess their true love and say goodbye, and this is really all too much for Sabrina Darling Davis to take in. The tears kept coming, and if you had asked Sabrina why she was so struck by this scene, she couldn't put it into words. Something deep down in her heart whispered to her that she would ultimately have to let Hottie go, and that thought alone made her sob uncontrollably. As much as she wanted to stay here with Hottie, in the perfect True Love bubble, she knew that the time was coming that she would have to let go.

Sabrina, deep down in the depths of her soul, knew that while she and Hottie had True Love and were perfect together, he still had a long painful path to face, a path full of fear and love lost. A path that can only be traveled on your own step by step. While Sabrina wanted to travel this path with her beloved Hottie, she knew that it wasn't her place.

Sabrina knew that she had not been there when love was lost and a marriage was ending. So to accompany him on the path of sorting it all out, coming to terms with the end, and healing from it in any REAL way, could not include her. And even though she knew she had to let go and let Hottie travel this path of brokenness on his own, she could not bear the thought of saying goodbye to her one and only True Love, which is why my dear girls, she was hysterical with tears.

The next day Hottie and Sabrina (Sahottie) came across a beautiful church located next to The Fancy Schmancy Hotel. As they wandered the streets hand in hand, they decided to go into this Church. When they walked in, Sabrina was in awe, huge cathedral ceiling, sparkling cream marble, and PEACE. A quiet solitude that enveloped you as soon as you walked in. So they there were, the only ones in the Church tucked away in a cozy pew staring at the beauty around them. It's not what she and Hottie said or didn't say in that Church, it was the feeling between them that said it all. It was this peace and feeling she felt next to him in this beautiful church that Sabrina would revisit many, many times to come.

If you asked her to put into words what that experience with Hottie was like, she wouldn't be able to. Rather it went beyond description, just a deep knowing that what they had was special, sacred even, and this was the perfect place to celebrate it and soak it all in. Sabrina wanted this tranquility, this peace, this love to last forever, but she knew it couldn't, not yet anyway. Hottie still had his ending to face, and later, Sabrina knew that there was a reason this was the last stop on the Sahottie train. A church, to pay reverence to what they both knew they had Sahottie =TRUE LOVE.

W.T.F.

The Fancy Schmancy weekend came to an end, and Fashionista called to invite Sabrina and Kat to the opening of a new swanky wine bar. Sabrina was excited to have a girl's night out and fill the girls in on the Hottie progress.

As the trio sipped their wine and people watched, Kat spotted two women that attend the same music class as her daughter, and they begin doing mommy talk. Kat politely introduces Fashionista and Sabrina to the Mommies and tells them that she lives vicariously through Sabrina and her hot new romance. The mommies are curious and want every detail of Sabrina's adventures with Hottie. The blonde mommy tells Sabrina she is glowing and that this sounds like true love for sure. She then asks Sabrina who the lucky man is and where he lives. Sabrina says his name is Hottie Fratatti and he is from Smallville, USA.

Blonde Mommy goes pale and her jaw drops to the floor. "Hottie Fratatti, from Smallville, USA??? That's your new boyfriend?????"

Sabrina looks at Kat feeling very weird. "Yes, why, do you know him?"

Blonde Mommy shakes her head disapprovingly. "Look Sabrina, I don't know how to tell you this but Hottie Fratatti is married. My husband and I had dinner with him and his wife last week."

"NOOO," Sabrina says, "he's separated in the midst of filing for divorce. You must be mistaken. It's been over for over a year, I met him a few months after they separated!"

Blonde Mommy grabs Sabrina's hand and squeezes it. "Sabrina, his wife's name is Wifey, and they have been married for fifteen years. Our daughters play together, and we attend the same church. He is very married and appears very happy. He's been lying to you…."

Sabrina feels her stomach churn. Kat grabs her other hand and tells Sabrina to sit down. Sabrina feels like an elephant is sitting on her chest. She can't catch her breathe, and she can taste the acid in her mouth that builds up when you are in shock.

"No, it can't be. He wouldn't lie to me…we're…we're in love…"

Blonde Mommy turns to Kat, "Kat, he's lying. I am friends with his wife, call her."

Kat tells Blonde Mommy to back off. Fashionista lights a cigarette and hands it to Sabrina. Sabrina takes a drag and feels like she is going to throw up. She puts her hand over her mouth and feels the wine start to come back up and burn her throat. She runs for the bathroom, but it's too late. She throws up right outside the bathroom door. Kat grabs a napkin and wipes Sabrina's mouth. Fashionista grabs Sabrina's purse, and they walk her to the door.

Sabrina hears Blonde Mommy in the background, "Sabrina, I'm sorry, he's a liar, you deserve better. This isn't good for you. Call his wife…he's married, definitely NOT separated or anywhere near a divorce."

Sabrina turns around to respond and feels her stomach churn again. "Let's get out of here," says Kat.

Sabrina can't speak. She can barely feel her legs. Married? Not separated? Happily married? OMG OMG OMG. Fashionista lights another cigarette and tries to calm Sabrina down.

"Sabrina, you never know, Blonde Mommy could be crazy and jealous. Let's just calm down. Just call him. Get the truth. Don't panic honey. It's going to be okay," Kat starts ranting. "What a prick! Taking you all over to wonderful hotels and buying you jewelry, you're his fucking mistress! I'm going to kill him!"

Sabrina feels numb. She wants to feel something, anything in this moment, and all she can feel is her heart pounding. Fashionista and Kat are ranting and raving, and their voices begin to sound like faint echoes in the distance. Kat insists Sabrina spend the night at her house since her hubbie is away on business, and her baby is with her mother. She makes Sabrina a cup of tea and begins to take the bobby pins out of Sabrina's hair. Sabrina still can't speak.

As Kat brushes Sabrina's hair she begins to speak, "Just call him, tell him about Blonde Mommy and get the truth. Get some sleep tonight, we will handle it in the morning."

Tomorrow morning, Hottie is coming to pick Sabrina up for yet another getaway, and while Sabrina had been looking forward to it all week, she is now nauseous. Kat hands her a sleeping pill and a shot of whiskey to calm her nerves. Sabrina, like a small obedient child, swallows the pill and does the shot.

She drifts off into sleep and awakes the next morning to her heart pounding out of her chest. Sabrina suddenly remembers the events of the night before. Blonde Mommy. Hottie and Wifey. Happily married. Her head starts to spin again. Kat stirs and very sternly says, "Go home, take a shower, wait until he picks you up and talk in person."

"Okay," Sabrina says. But she knows this is far from okay.

Wifey

Sabrina opens the door and Hottie gives her a big grin and smacks a kiss on her lips. Sabrina feels her hands shaking. "What?" Hottie says. "Sabrina, you look pale…What is it???"

Sabrina takes a deep breathe, looks Hottie right in the eye and says with her voice quivering, "Is there something you want to tell me?"

Hottie shakes his head, "What are you talking about…?"

"TELL ME THE TRUTH. NOWWWWWWWW."

Sabrina does not recognize her own voice. It sounds primal and scary. Hottie starts to fidget and his pupils get huge. Sabrina remembers an episode of America's Most Wanted. When the person starts to fidget and shift their eyes, they are lying.

"AHHH, ERRRR, UMMMM," Hottie stammers. Sabrina stays silent. "I, errrrr, what is going on with you Sabrina, talk to ME!!!?????"

Sabrina speaks in bullet points, "Wine Bar opening, Blonde Mommy, Wifey, not even close to a divorce."

Hottie falls to his knees, wraps his arms around her legs, and begins to weep. Sabrina wants to kick him while he's down but somehow restrains herself.

"We were, we ARE having problems. I have been unhappy for years. I met you and I had to know you, had to see if this was real. I couldn't risk losing you. I LOVE YOU. I just can't leave right now, my daughter needs me. Please, please forgive me. I am so sorry Sabrina." Now he is shaking and crying and looks pathetic, and as mad as Sabrina is, she wants to fall into his arms and pretend this is all a bad dream.

Sabrina feels rage well up in her chest. "How could you…how could you put me in that position? How could you lie to me about this?" Sabrina is shaking her head and staring at Hottie wondering who this man is that she has been sharing her life and her bed with. "GET OUT," she screams. "GET THE FUCK OUT, YOU ASS-HOLE!!!!!"

Sabrina pushes him with super-human strength into the wall. Her mirror falls to the floor and shatters into a million pieces. Now Hottie's sobbing, and Sabrina is sobbing, and this whole scene looks like a bad Lifetime movie.

"Sabrina please, I can't lose you, please, you have to understand, its complicated…"

Now Sabrina can't see beyond her tears. She slaps him across the face as hard as she can, which feels strangely good, and pushes him out the door. "GET OUT AND LEAVE ME ALONE! I HATE YOU!!!!!"

Door slams. Silence. Sabrina falls to the floor and leans against the door. She puts her head between her legs and takes some deep breathes to calm herself down. She starts to dry heave as a million questions go through Sabrina's mind all at once. Was this a joke? A dream? How could I be so stupid…How could I rush into this soooo fast? How could I put myself in this position…OMG OMG OMG.

And then she hears Him.

"Shhhhhhh. I AM HERE."

Love, God.

Sabrina can't even answer Him. She just shakes her head and wishes she could disappear.

Goodbye Hottie

Hottie blows Sabrina's phone up with apologies, promises, tears, and remorse. Sabrina makes Kat listen to them and delete them so she doesn't have to hear it. Kat does some investigating and finds out that Mr. and Mrs. Hottie Fratatti are happily married and building a new home next door to Kat's sister-in-law, who thankfully, lives hours away.

The next few weeks are filled with anger, tears, nausea and confusion. Sabrina could barely function at work, and each day she felt like she was in a deep dark fog. She felt very suddenly, silent. The Sabrina who talked incessantly, dived into life like a cannonball and laughed maybe even cackled loudly was very quiet. The sound of the radio, or TV even, seemed too loud and too overwhelming, it was silence and solitude that she needed. And she knew, from personal and professional experience, that if she did not stop to deal with this sadness, anger, and pain, she would do what it seemed most people did, avoid pain and replace it with cheap substitutes. Sabrina knew that she could not drink, smoke, shop, or even flirt her way through this. She had to stop and pause…

Too often, she had counseled people who refused to face the pain of betrayal or love lost. They would instead, pull the blame card out of the deck and give Sabrina a long winded tale of how they were cheated and scorned from THE ONE who had screwed up their life. She found it appalling that very few were willing to sit in the wing chair and say, I take full responsibility for my part, and here's how I contributed to the problem, and I will learn from this and do it better next time.

No, too many used the shields of anger and bitterness to protect themselves from ever having to look deep within. Why was pain so hard to face? Why didn't people realize that it is this very pain that helps people grow, learn and change for the better?? And sometimes, when Sabrina would push her clients to face the pain, they would react with anger…Don't you know what she/he did to me??? He/she ruined my life???? And Sabrina wanted to shout back, NO, YOU ARE LETTING THEM RUIN YOUR LIFE!!! WAKE UP!!!!!!!!

This is how Sabrina knew she would have to deal with saying goodbye to Hottie, wide awake one step at time, feeling the pain and facing it head on with courage and a willingness to learn. And as she tried to work and listen and help her clients, all Sabrina really wanted to do was crawl up into the wing chair next to her clients and say, "Guess what…I was in love, or at least I thought I was, and I had to let it go, and I am so very sad right now, so very very sad. And I can't tell you everything will be okay, or that you will survive what you are going through, because I am not sure I will, and you may want to get a new therapist…because I am just not sure if I will ever recover."

Of course, Sabrina didn't do this. Rather, she tried her best, to listen and be there in their pain, wide awake and fully present, all the while thinking and feeling her own deep pain and sorrow. It was during these first few weeks, that clients would for no explanation, forget they had appointments set up all together, and Sabrina would relish the extra hour just to sit alone, curled up in the wing chair and think, and, most of all, feel. It was at these moments she would find herself walking very quietly down the hall to her mother's office. The mixed smell of her mother's perfume, soap and powder was enough to calm her down and comfort her for a moment. Ahhh, the delicious Mommy smell. It was in these first few weeks that Sabrina would find herself taking comfort in the smell of her Mommy, the one and only person, who could make her feel better.

There Sabrina sat, curled up in a chair, in her mother's office, staring at this woman that had always been there. Sabrina's mom was a woman of timeless elegance, ever flowing wisdom, all know-ing, all feeling, woman of beauty and youth whose eyes, despite any years, danced with excitement and wonderment. It was her mother, who would hold her up during those first few weeks. It wasn't so much what her mother said, it was what she didn't say that mat-tered most. She was Sabrina's mother, the woman that her knew her better than anyone, the woman who knew what was best for her daughter, based purely on the gift of mother's intuition she knew that while Hottie lied about his circumstances, and whoever it was he pretended to be, Sabrina had fallen for him.

What Sabrina didn't know as that her mom had been quietly watching and taking in every detail as she watched her daughter fall for Hottie. And what her mother was struck by most of all, upon meeting Hottie, is that he loved her daughter. She could see it in his eyes, and the way he held Sabrina close. As she watched from the sidelines, she saw her daughter fall more and more every day, deeply settled into herself. Whatever it was Sahottie had, she had seen it first hand. No matter how much she wanted to protect her daughter from hurt and love lost, deep down, Sabrina's mom knew that her daughter was forever changed from this experience in the best of ways. And instead of doubting or cursing it, she was go-ing to fully embrace this experience of love that had changed her youngest child. While she secretly hoped Hottie was dying without her daughter and the light of her presence in his life, what she really wished for, above all, is that her darling daughter would always, no matter what, feel the peace and love of a mother's heart cheering Sabrina along every step of the way.

Sabrina's mom encouraged her to take this experience and use it for good. Instead of cursing Hottie and his lies, she pushed Sa-brina to consider what she had learned, felt and how she had grown. And while Sabrina wanted to be bitter and focus on what a prick Hottie was, the truth was, she missed him, or whoever it was that she had fallen in love with. One day they were going away for a weekend and the next day, POOF, gone. Over. Done. Finished. GAME OVER. This was, for sure, the hardest part to accept. No more Sahottie. Goodbye Forever.

Are you There God, It's me, Sabrina?

She went to bed that night dreaming of Hottie, they were letting go of one another and crying and holding on to each other for dear life but could never fully let go. And every time they tried to, they ended up clinging to each other more tightly. When Sabrina woke up the next morning, she was in a deep dark fog. But the thing about this fog is she felt a peace, the kind of peace that surpasses your logic and simply takes your heart and wraps it in a warm cozy blanket. Sabrina knew that this warmth, in the midst of the cold, deep, dark fog, was the one and only True Love, God Himself.

Sabrina knew what this meant. Every time she had come to a crossroad in her life, God would send peace to show her the path to choose. And the peace He would send was beyond her ability to analyze, rationalize, therapize, or even frostasize. No matter how hard she tired to escape it or even deny it, the path was always clearly marked with peace. And this is how Sabrina would always choose her path, the one of deep, unable to ever capture with words ...PEACE.

So, it was on this very foggy, peaceful morning that Sabrina decided she would let Hottie go. With her eyes filled with tears she began to write an email:

> Dear Hottie Fratatti,
>
> I know I have to let you go, and I just did. (Enter Tears) I am saying goodbye. I know I will be okay, grow stronger and maybe even love again. (SOB!) I can only speak for myself and know that I conducted myself with honesty throughout our relationship. You cannot say the same. I have to move on, let go and be free. I miss you. I miss us. I miss it all. I am

sure, you miss me.

Be a good father and live your life with honesty. Stop fucking around and deal with your baggage. Talk to God and get your life together. I pray you don't do this to any other women, although, I secretly think you might if you haven't already. Do not call me, leave me alone, and let me move on with my life.

Now I am going to be the bigger person here. God Bless you. Goodbye.

Love, Sabrina

As Sabrina pushed the send button and got ready for work, streams of tears came down her face. And no matter how hard she tried to stop them, they kept coming. As she pulled herself together and courageously walked up the steps to her office in tears, she tried to compose herself to face the day, a day of hearing other people's pain and problems in the midst of her own pain, she stopped to check her email. Much to her surprise, but not at all really, there was an email from Hottie Fratatti. Written, and I swear to God, at the same exact time that morning, Sabrina had written him.

Dear Sabrina,

I love you and always will. Please know that I will miss your lips, face, body, smile and eyes, although not your various nasal sprays.

(Damn it, Hottie was even funny in the midst of heartbreak.)

I have never in my life had an experience like I did with you, and I know I never will. I know now that love exists for me, and it is with you. You are my best friend, and I will think about you every day. I cherished our time together and am so sorry I hurt you. My heart aches for you and always will.

> Please think of me with smiles, not tears, and please remember our times with joy. Please know my thoughts are always with you and always will be. I want the best for you and know I have to stop contacting you. I am so very sorry. Please forgive me.
>
> Love, Hottie Fratatti

This is what Sabrina would always remember, without words, without begging, pleading or hanging on, she and Hottie had let each other go at the exact same moment in time. There was no way that morning she knew she had an email waiting. And as tragic as this all was, Sabrina felt deeply comforted. Deeply comforted that no matter what happened or happens, she will be okay. As much as she wanted to hate Hottie, despise him, maybe even torture him, she forgave him. Maybe that's the purest form of love we have to offer, forgiveness.

Sabrina knew that if she didn't come to that place of letting Hottie go, the rage and anger would eat her alive and deaden her heart. Hottie belonged to someone else. He was not hers, Hottie belonged to Wifey.

> Dear God,
>
> WTF. I took this way too fast and feel like such an idiot. I should have done my homework, taken my time, and not been so trusting with Hottie.
>
> Please help me get through this. Please help me to move forward. Please help me to learn from this.
>
> (and here was the prayer that was the toughest to get out…) And God, please bless Wifey and Hottie's relationship. Heal it.
>
> Love, Sabrina

> Dear Sabrina,

I LOVE YOU. I AM WTH YOU.
Love, God

ACHEY BREAKY HEART

The next few weeks were cold, gray and rainy. It was if God Himself knew that bright sun and warmth would be too much for Sabrina too handle. It's not that she never wanted to see the sunshine, or experience love again, it was more that she knew that she wasn't ready for a bright sunny day, not yet anyway.

Here's the thing about grief and heartbreak. It crops up on you at the most random, unexpected moments. Sabrina would be in aisle 9 of the grocery store, the organic low sodium section (salt made her face bloat to new levels) and while feeling perfectly stable, strong, collected and FINE, she would be staring at the sodium content of the label and burst into tears. She quickly learned that grief and loss were like swimming in the ocean on a warm summer day. You can be perfectly content enjoying the water and the sunshine, and BOOM, a wave hits…

Right then and there, you have to make a decision that you will either fight the wave or ride it into the shore, but no matter what, you are going to have to face it. So whether it was in the grocery store, gas station, or shopping for a new dress, Sabrina would find herself overcome with waves of emotion having to very quickly disappear from the public eye and let herself ride with the emotion to cry.

When the tears hit, they were sometimes so unexpected that she would often panic and head for the nearest dressing room, bathroom, or home, just so she could confront the waves of sadness head on. It was at these times that she would feel her stomach drop to her knees and the tears come with big, huge waves of sadness. And while she wanted to override each wave of sadness, she knew, from her experience watching countless clients sit in her office and try to run from pain and sadness, she had to ride with the waves and acknowledge that the pain of losing Hottie was deep and real, and no amount of denial or avoiding was going to get her elsewhere.

So as Sabrina faced the reality of life without Hottie, she found herself very sensitive. Like brought to her knees in tears when anyone, close to her or not, showed KINDNESS. She would find herself trying to ease into a lane of traffic, and a stranger would smile and give her the "ALL CLEAR GO" sign, and she would start to cry at the gesture of kindness. Or, she would be in line to check out at the grocery store and the cashier and bag person would be overly nice to the point that Sabrina would start to get teary. Or, even more heart wrenching, a client would walk into her office and tell Sabrina, with tears of gratitude, what her wisdom and belief in them had done to make them better, and Sabrina would find herself in a puddle of gratitude and love, with a side of pain, sprinkle of sadness and grief.

It was these random, or maybe not so random, acts of kindness and pure love of people that would comfort Sabrina in the weeks to come. And when Sabrina would retreat to the comforts of home, all she really wanted to do was call Hottie to tell him about her day, hold him close, and feel him curled up next to her, arms holding her tight with his lips upon her forehead. Often she would come home from a day of working, shopping, or running errands and find herself overwhelmed wanting to talk to Hottie and let him know exactly what she felt. Sometimes she would talk outloud, as if he were right next to her in the car, or home with her in her apartment. She would crawl into bed and tell him every detail of her day hoping that somehow this ache in her heart would go away.

Sabrina Davis, Party of One?

As the weeks wore on, Preppy and Lyssie called to invite her to a charity ball. Preppy and Lyssie were a 20 something couple who had been dating since high school. They had unbelievable drive and ambition to succeed in life and though forever hard workers and driven in their careers, they also knew how to have fun and enjoy a good time. At first their friendship was one of, hey neighbor, join us for a beer. As they spent time together getting to know one another, it was one of those friendships that clicked and grew comfortably. Often they would shout to Sabrina from their terrace, COME OVER, JITTERBUG!!!!! And it was in Preppy and Lyssie's kitchen that Sabrina learned the jitterbug.

They would dance until the wee hours of the morning laughing hysterically because Sabrina, no matter how hard she tried, was always one beat off. And eventually she would yell "Fuck it!" and break into her own free style Sabrina Darling Davis moves. This would only make Preppy and Lyssie more hysterical. Sabrina had learned that to test any man of interest and possible potential, she would have to see if he could survive a night of jitterbugging in her dear friend's kitchen. On one such evening, Sabrina bravely brought Mr. Green. An architect who designed and implemented H.O.V. lanes across the country. And Sabrina, too embarrassed to asked thought, what the hell is huOV? (H.O.V)

So, attempting to save herself of this embarrassment, she quickly headed for the bathroom and called her sister Belle. "What is an H.O.V. lane? That's what this guy does for a living."

Belle, being related to Sabrina said, "WHAT??? HuOV????" Then Belle shouted out to her brilliant, like so smart its scary, husband, Dr. Heart, "Honey what is a HuOV lane??"

To which Dr. Heart laughed out loud and said, "You guys

are kidding right….H.O.V., high occupancy vehicle, on highways to keep traffic moving for people that carpool." OHHHH. Right thought Sabrina, of course. Carpool?? And this is when she knew her days were numbered with Mr. Green.

Sabrina could think of nothing worse than having to engage in small talk with colleagues first thing in the morning. And while she did recycle and turn off her lights, there was no freakin way she was going to carpool to get in the HuOV lane. Poor Mr. Green sat in Preppy and Lyssie's kitchen looking bored out of his mind, never ever once getting up to learn the jitterbug. But Sabrina was okay with this, she was ov-Hoova it. Carpooling was not in the cards for her, like not even close. So long Mr. Green….

As Sabrina got ready for the charity ball, she tried to feel excited. She was for the first time in weeks, going out for an evening on the town. While she knew she should put a smile on her face and a gorgeous dress on, Sabrina wasn't feeling it. What she really wanted was to be putting on a gorgeous dress and head to the ball with Hottie, but Sabrina had to remind herself that he was Wifey's. Right, married, Wifey.

That night when her date rang to pick her up, it was not Hottie, but Fashionista, who as usual, looked stunning in "The Designer" dress. The rain was pouring down, and as Sabrina and Fashionista walked to the ball, they tried to keep their umbrellas straight. They would burst into fits of giggles as the wind turned them inside out. It felt good to laugh, thought Sabrina, as she walked into the ball. She was ready to have a good time, even if her mind was fixed on Hottie.

Preppie, Lyssie, Fashionista, Sabrina, and Preppie's parents, Moosh and Pierre, met at the bar to have a cocktail and catch up. Moosh and Sabrina had shared a special connection from the day they met. Moosh was the type of person that would squeeze you close and pour out love as soon as she met you whether it was a first time meeting, or the hundredth time, you were going to have a love fest. A dazzling smile and spirit full of love and light, Moosh had forever been in Sabrina's corner when it came to love.

So that night, when Moosh asked about Hottie, Sabrina told her about Wifey. Lyssie remarked, "Wow, how could you NOT know about Wifey??? What were you thinking???"

Ouch. Sting. Big-time Ouch. Sabrina wanted to sink into a hole and die. The shame rose up from her feet and she suddenly felt two inches tall. Moosh grabbed her arm and squeezed it.

"Sabrina, you will heal, move on, and fall in love again."

Sabrina found her mind screaming, was Hottie a cruel joke? What was I thinking? Was it True Love? Was it a game of passion and romance, just lust? Am I a fool?????

As the ball ended, Fashionista insisted they all go out dancing, but Sabrina politely declined and headed home, feeling anxiety and doubt course through her mind and body. As she walked down Main Street the rain poured down and the wind picked up. Sabrina's umbrella turned completely inside out, and she began to get soaked. She pulled her pashmina over her head to stay dry and as she stepped off the curb to cross the street, she stepped into a huge wet ice cold puddle (in brand new sparkly black shoes).

And that was it, the tears came streaming down her face, big huge crocodile tears, and as a group of collegiates walked past her talking loudly and laughing, ready to begin an evening of fun, they saw Sabrina and became suddenly quiet. It was if they too, could feel her pain, and it was too much to watch. But Sabrina didn't even notice, she cried all the way home with her pashmina over her head, feet soaked to the bone, and heart breaking into pieces every step of the way. As she walked into her dark, silent apartment she felt somewhat comforted. As if the solitude and darkness agreed that what she felt was beyond words, and they were willing to sit with her, and comfort her, and be with her, in the doubt and pain of a broken heart.

She dropped her purse, pashmina, earrings, shoes, and one by one, began leaving a trail of clothes and accessories as she made her way to her bedroom. And as she climbed into her bed alone and in the darkness, she pulled the covers to her chin and sobbed.

GIRLPOWER

Sabrina finally fell asleep that night and when she awoke the next day she felt somehow cleansed of all the pain, doubt and anxiety that had so deeply plagued her the night before. She was relieved that today she was going to enjoy a day of beauty and relaxation. Hair done for color and trim, then off to "The Spa" for a massage, sauna, and parafarrin treatment for her hands and feet. Sabrina knew she needed this day of pampering and as she sipped her coffee that morning and looked out onto her terrace to see the busyness of the day begin, she realized it was Hottie's birthday. And rather than feel all sad and begin the tears again, Sabrina silently wished him a happy birthday from her heart and prayed that he would have the best year of his life. As she prayed that prayer, she felt the sadness begin to lift for the first time in weeks.

The heaviness and pain seemed to release their grip from Sabrina's chest and heart, and she knew right then and there, on Hottie's birthday of all days, that she was going to be just fine. The Sabrina who bounced through life with joy and laughter would make her way back into the world, and she would take this experience and use it for good and only good.

Sabrina was tired of feeling sad and knew it was time to buck up. The only thing she could do was to be thankful for the experience and move forward with courage and hope. And of course, Sabrina knew that there would still be moments of tears and sadness and probably even anger to push through, but something had shifted from the inside of her soul. Sabrina was ready to take this experience and find a way to better herself, and everyone around her, because of it.

As Sabrina began the chilly cold walk to the hair salon, she began to come to some conclusions about this experience with Hottie.

While the entire ending was an absolute nightmare, Sabrina knew that after years of doubting her ability to engage in a healthy loving relationship the days of questioning herself and altering her personality to participate in someone else's dysfunction were gone. Hottie had shown her that she was worthy of having the love she wanted, no settling, no altering, no anxiety, just peace and love.

Never mind the fact that he lied to her and led her down a path of heartbreak, no matter what, she knew this experience had grown her confidence in herself, and she knew that she was never ever going to settle or question herself again, except that now she would have every date undergo a lie detector test and fingerprint screening. Other than those two minor things, she was better off for having met Hottie.

Sabrina wondered how many women have been through something similar. Duped into a fantasy and boom, one day you run into a Blonde Mommy and your bubble of perfect love is gone. Why, as women, do we judge, criticize and gossip about each other and our mistakes in life?? Why do we find it so hard to encourage and build one another up to make good decisions and live in truth?? Too often, we take the road of slander and gossip rather than compassion and encouragement.

As Sabrina begin her day of beauty and relaxation, she decided that it was time to get her ass in gear and begin to live again. She was tired of feeling mopey, teary, and depressed. Every time Kat called her first words were, "Are you okay…????"

She was certain her friends and family were getting tired of the woe is me bit. So, with a kick in the ass, Sabrina made a conscious decision that day to move forward and live again. Maybe even, love again. And while the idea of a date was somewhat appealing Sabrina couldn't help but think it was time to take on a project that empowered women to be healthy and wise in relationships.

She wanted to craft a message that empowered women to work

together and support one another instead of competing and belittling each other every step of the way. Right there on the massage table as she felt her entire body relax and unwind...BOOM. KAPOW. POP. She felt the flutter of her heart and enthusiasm build and a burst of energy that can only come from inspiration. The creative enthusiasm that generates life changing ideas was here, knocking on Sabrina's heart, loudly, clearly, and ENTHUSIASTICALLY. Sabrina knew, right then and there, naked on a massage table of all places, exactly how to use this HOTTIE debacle for good...Drum roll please...

LADIES AND GENTLEMAN: ON THIS VERY COLD CHILLY DAY, ON HOTTIE FRATATTI's BIRTHDAY OF ALL DAYS, WE ARE PLEASED TO ANNOUNCE THE ARRIVAL OF THE ONE AND ONLY...... GIRLPOWER!!!!!!!!!!!!!!!!!!!

Applause. Cheers. Hoorays. GO GIRLPOWER!!!!

GIRLPOWER is: The belief that every girl deserves to feel loved, accepted, beautiful, talented, unique and FABULOUS. It's not about being perfect, it's about being PERFECTLY YOU.

Day after day, women of all ages would make their way into Sabrina's office doubting themselves from head to toe. If only I were "prettier, skinnier, smarter, blonder, whiter, darker, stronger, taller, shorter, if only I were NOT ME then it would be okay"... ATTENTION GIRLS! NO MORE!! From now on it's GIRLPOWER.

The Hottie debacle did result in some good and had given Sabrina the courage to grab a hold of her heart from the depths of her soul and say "ENOUGH. I LOVE YOU, SABRINA DAVIS, AND I ACCEPT YOU. YOU ARE GOOD ENOUGH!"

That was how she was going to use the message of True Love. Imagine, thought Sabrina, if women everywhere, girls, tweens, teens, women, ladies, chicks, broads,....ACCEPTED AND LOVED THEMSELVES!!!! Imagine a world where women help and encourage one another to love and accept themselves instead of competing and comparing themselves to one another.

What if, one by one, girls everywhere would hear the message of GIRLPOWER and women would STOP once and for all looking in the mirror and feeling the shame of not being good enough! Imagine all girls looking into the mirror and smiling and saying, "you GO GIRL!!! YOU ARE ENOUGH!!!"

This was True GIRLPOWER!!!!

Sabrina could hardly finish the massage she was so excited, bursting with energy, ready to get the message out.

> Dear God,
>
> Sabrina Davis here. Guess what???? I have an amazing idea, it's called GIRLPOWER and it's based on LOVE and acceptance and I think it can change the WORLD! WAHHOOOOOO.
>
> Love, Sabrina

> Dear Sabrina,
>
> God here, Hellloooo, who do you think gave you the idea????
>
> Love, God

Ohhh, right. Divine Inspiration. Thanks a million God. GIRL-POWER Rocks, pass it on!

As Sabrina headed home from her massage she knew exactly how to get this message out. She was going to write a book. Sabrina Darling Davis, former Barbie shoe chewing, aspiring actress, karaoke singer, genius therapist, was about to add best-selling author of *GIRLPOWER* to her list.

She dusted off her laptop that was given to her by her father, Sylvia, over a year ago. Sabrina did not even have internet access in her apartment because she really had no interest in it. Sure, she could email and Google the new guy she was getting set up with, but that was about the only thing she cared to do. When she figured out how to turn the laptop on and plug in the mouse (she didn't like the touch pad thing because it never seemed to go where Sabrina wanted it to go), she began to type.

Fast, furious, pouring out of her heart Sabrina could not stop. She had a message of love and she wanted to get it out to women everywhere ASAP. And this is how it went for the next few weeks… Sabrina would come home from work and type away until the wee hours of the morning. All she could think about, talk about, dream about was *GIRLPOWER.*

Sabrina had even written on a bright pink index card with a black Sharpe marker, *GIRLPOWER,* by, Sabrina Davis, New York Times bestseller, born on this cold blustery day, which just so happens to be Hottie Fratatti's birthday. And every day when Sabrina sat down to write, she would put this bright pink card in front of her to keep the vision burning bright. Brushing her teeth and washing her face became a nuisance. Friday and Saturday nights rather than hit the town with friends, Sabrina was content to write her heart out all weekend long. While Sabrina knew she should ease up and join the world again, she couldn't do it. Nope, *GIRLPOWER* was her mission and nothing else, not even flirting with boys, (GASP!) seemed to matter.

Pages and pages poured out of Sabrina and she knew if this was going to be big she would have to save her book and back it up. So Sabrina put in the call to Kat, who was a technology wizard, and naively asked, "What kind of floppy disk do I need to save this?"

Kat was in hysterics. "Floppy disk?" replied Kat, "That is so early 90's, where have you been????!!!" And right then and there, dear Kat became Sabrina's technology expert, plugging in and saving and saving and downloading, and printing, and doing whatever it took to keep *GIRLPOWER* alive and well.

As the weeks flew by, Kat and Fashionista, rather than beg and plea Sabrina to come join them on the town, would arrive at her door wine in hand to sit down and read *GIRLPOWER*. They knew the only way they were going to ever see their dear friend again was if they came to her.

"Geez," Fashionista exclaimed when she walked through the door, "When is the last time you cleaned???"

Sabrina, who was usually a clean freak, nothing ever out of place, had become a complete slob. She barely had time to go to the bathroom lest she lose this creative vibe coursing through her body, let alone vacuum and Windex (which she loved to do by the way). There was nothing like the sparkle of a sink that had been freshly Windexed, and yes, Sabrina was aware of the chemicals in Windex, but that was what gave her sink the sparkly look, and she was not about to give up the sparkle for clean air.

So, with Fashionista Windexing away and Kat drinking away, Sabrina could not help but think about how, whenever she had been introduced to a writer at a cocktail party, or some other social gathering, she always felt they were odd, and frankly, very weird. She finally could understand it. She had become so absorbed and engulfed in writing *GIRLPOWER* that she too was getting weird. Like the thought of participating in real life was just too disrupting to Sabrina's creative FLOW. (Chime the peace gong please.) Kat and Fashionista, bless their dear souls, jumped into Sabrina's world, rolled their sleeves up and begin to edit and work on the book with Sabrina. Kat would read new excerpts and burst out with laughter cheering Sabrina on, while spell checking too, of course. Sabrina found this whole right click on mouse to spell check just a complete waste of creative energy.

Fashionista would sip her wine, read out loud and take over the keyboard editing for Sabrina. Sabrina was amazed and grateful that *GIRLPOWER*, while being birthed to the world, was taking place in her kitchen. Her two dear and precious friends were embracing Sabrina's vision with enthusiasm and love and doing whatever it took to help their dear friend share it with the world. *GIRLPOWER* was alive and well in Sabrina's heart and home-unbelievable!!!!!!!!!!!!!!

Sabrina began to practice *GIRLPOWER* in her counseling practice. When adolescents or women of any age came in to her office and began the list of things they hated about themselves, Sabrina would stop them right there and have them close their eyes and say the awful things they were saying about themselves back to them.

"You are ugly, you are worthless, you are fat, you are stupid, you are not good enough..." Tears would fall down their cheeks as one by one, these precious women began to realize the self abuse they were engaging in constantly with their negative, hateful, not ever good enough thoughts about themselves. Sabrina would then have each woman really focus on what she did appreciate about herself, or what she desperately wished to feel. Sabrina would send them off with a pink index card of positive self affirmations:

I am good enough.
I am worthy of love.
I am beautiful.
I am unique.
I am talented.
I love my body and see it with eyes of beauty.
I walk with my head held high.
I am full of confidence.
I choose to love and accept myself today.

She would have the girls repeat messages of love to themselves daily, out loud, right in front of the mirror. It was amazing to see the transformation, right here, in her little office, as her clients began to get the message of self acceptance and love. Many women would find themselves walking away from relationships that were full of negativity and control. Some of the adolescent girls

Sabrina counseled began to really focus on their studies and unique talents instead of spending every waking moment trying to impress the "guy" or be in the popular clique.

Sabrina was in awe as women began to walk into her office with a sparkle and new found confidence, this *GIRLPOWER*stuff was real and life changing!!!! She even tried it on a few men-ha! Boy Power! But for now, her focus was on girls and only girls. Boy Power would have its day, but first things first (besides we all know women really are the wiser ones and that's where real change starts, pass it on…)

So while Sabrina wrote like a mad woman and practiced her *GIRLPOWER* theories on her clients, the world continued to spin and Thanksgiving was fast approaching.

Bags packed and Jackie O shades in hand, Sabrina headed to Florida to spend the week with her family. Lots of laughs, great food, and cloudless sunny days, it was just what Sabrina needed to refuel and unwind. And as they sat around the dinner table with a beautiful view of the ocean and a pink and purple sunset, one by one each family member took a turn to say what they were especially thankful for.

When it was Sabrina's turn she said with a smirk on her face and a twinkle in her eye, "Well, you may all want to rethink your wardrobe choices, because when you are in the audience to lend support for my Oprah appearance, you will want to look your best!"

That's right! Sabrina Davis was thankful for the fact that she had a best seller on its way to the world, and Oprah would, of course, be calling to invite Sabrina to share her message of *GirlPower*.

Her family laughed as her dad, Sylvia, said, "What planet do you live on???"

And Sabrina smiled and replied, "LOVE. I live on the planet LOVE." Everyone at the same time made gagging sounds and her brother pretended to pass out from the cheesiness ultimate queer bait of his sister's statement.

But Sabrina didn't care. She was in love with LOVE and ready to inspire anyone and everyone with her message of hope. She had seen the dramatic changes self love and acceptance had made in her life, and the lives of all the women who came to see her for counseling. No doubt, this Love stuff was the best antidepressant around... Goodbye Prozac, hello LOVE and Self acceptance. Side effects are: peace, beauty, joy, light heartedness and serenity...what could be better! Pass it on......

Sun and fun over, and Sabrina once again headed back to the routine of seeing clients all day and writing all night. Kat and Fashionista were calling non-stop to see if she was alive and how the book was going. And as everyone prepared for the holiday season, Sabrina was in her own little, but soon to be BIG, season of *Girl-Power*.

At her counseling practice, one of her clients who weighed over 500 pounds at the beginning of her counseling, began to shed pounds, exercise, eat right, and most importantly, she began to LOVE herself. Sabrina could barely believe the transformation of confidence in Dee. Her entire face began to lift and glow in a way that was remarkable. When Sabrina first began counseling Dee, she could barely make eye contact or hold her head up she was so ashamed of herself. And now she was walking into Sabrina's office with a bright smile and slowly shrinking body. This true *GIRL-POWER* example fueled Sabrina's creativity as she came to the finish line of her message. On the cold blustery day of December 1, Sabrina proudly wrote the words...THE END.

The end of a time where women will shame themselves incessantly with negative messages of self loathing and unacceptance. *GIRLPOWER* has arrived and is "The Beginning." The beginning of a time when women will once and for all take a stand to love and accept themselves and one another. *GIRLPOWER* is HERE!...

PASS IT ON...

Tadaaaa……it was finished! Sabrina felt a mixture of sadness and excitement all rolled into one. Tears fell from her face as she wrote the final words to *GirlPower*. She was sad that the project she threw her heart and soul to was in some ways coming to an end, but excited at the endless possibilities that existed once the message of *GIRLPOWER* was out. You see my dear girls, *GIRLPOWER* had kept Sabrina from feeling sad and missing Hottie. And while there were many a night she would find herself clutching the body pillow next to her pretending it was Hottie right next to her to keep her warm, *GIRLPOWER* had kept Sabrina sane and alive. She found herself feeling scared that she had come to the end of this project and that sadness and grief would once again, come knocking on her door. Sabrina found herself wanting to call Hottie Fratatti and say, "Guess what? I wrote a book and I think it's going to be huge!!!"

But Sabrina knew in her heart that she could not contact Hottie and in some ways, Sabrina had to believe deep down that Hottie was thinking of her, and believing that his Darling was doing wonderful successful things. That was what Hottie would always tell Sabrina, that she was going to be a huge success at whatever she did in her career and life in general. And Sabrina knew that had she never had the experience and heartbreak with Hottie, that *GIRLPOWER* would not exist.

So for this, she was thankful for the lying, deceitful jerk that she fell hard and fast for. Hours and hours of editing began as Sabrina gave copies to her family and friends. Most of the reviews she got were positive and encouraging. Phew, but this didn't surprise Sabrina at all. She had known since the day she started writing *GirlPower* that this was way bigger than her. She knew this message had come from her pal, God, and that He was using her as the mouth piece, which was fine with Sabrina because she did know, and was often told, that she had a big mouth.

Next step, publisher. Fashionista had a very famous relative who was a publisher for a huge firm in the City. Fashionista got in touch with her and boom, *GIRLPOWER* was sent, on pink paper of course, to the big City for review. As the next few weeks rolled by Sabrina desperately wanted to chew on her nails, Barbie shoes, pens, anything! But she knew she just had to wait it out and believe that *GIRLPOWER* would come into the world, in some fashion, hopefully ISTA, or another.

And then the call came.

Fashionista (who had become Sabrina's editor and secret agent) called: THEY LOVE IT!

Sabrina: NOOOOO!!!!!!!!!!!!!!!!

Fashionista: YES!!!!!!!!!!!!! They are GA GAAAAAAAAA over it and you and I, my friend, are headed to the big City to meet with them to start negotiations for a contract and marketing!!!!!!!!!!!!!!!!!

Sabrina: OMG!!!!!!!!!!!!! What should I wear????

Fashionista: No worries, I am on it. Something FAB-U-LOUSAHHHH.

So there they were on the train headed to the big meeting. Fashionista had designed a suit for Sabrina that was a jade/turquoise raw silk, to bring out her eyes of course, hip city chic with one of Fashionista's handbags, that she had, of course, designed on her own. And it was my dear girls, just as Fashionista had promised Fab-u-LOUSA!

As they entered the building and took the elevator to the top floor, Sabrina grabbed Fashionista's hand and squeezed it with tears of gratitude in her eyes. "Thank you."

Fashionista squeezed back. "*GirlPower*."

An hour later, contract in negotiations and Sabrina was what they called "The next Big Thing." *GIRLPOWER* was here and about to be broadcast to THE WORLD!

She and Fashionista headed out for celebratory drinks and hopefully, as Fashionista had promised flirting with adorable city boys. Sabrina was actually feeling somewhat human again and ready to flirt, maybe even have a good old lusty make out just to get her back in the game.

That night as they sipped their drinks, Fashionista captured every man's eye in the room, and Sabrina, no matter how hard she tried, could not get into the meet and greet mood. She felt, if anything, strangely humbled. She suddenly felt very honored that she, Sabrina Davis, had written a message, truly inspired from her heart, that had been accepted and received with applause.

It was all too much to take in at once and all this emotion was making her feel like she wanted to disappear from the bright lights and big city to breathe and get her head on straight. And as the very handsome and charming "friend" of the guy who was chatting up Fashionista moved in to talk to Sabrina, she had, OMG, Gasp, no interest. Zero. Natta. Zilch.

> Dear God,
> Sabrina Davis here with an urgent message. I have no urge to drink, smoke or flirt. AM I IN HELL???????????? Get back immediately.
> Love, Sabrina

It's not that Sabrina wasn't interested in flirting with men anymore, or in some desperate can't get over "The Best Ever Guy who happened to be married" mode, it was more that she felt had had the real deal. The Hottie she fell in love with (whoever he was) was what she wanted, and she did not have the energy to try and engage with someone who was so clearly not for her and so clearly, NOT REAL.

"The Friend" was talking incessantly about his huge career on Wall Street, and his big amazing apartment, and how successful he was, and how he could take Sabrina and Fashionista out for a "real" night in the city to all "The Places" with "The People." Instead of feeling excited and breathless over all the charm, Sabrina felt bored and exhausted. More exhausted for him, than for herself.

He was making an all out sales pitch to Sabrina about how wonderful he was, and he was so busy selling himself to Sabrina, that he had not once even noticed that she was staring into her drink and secretly dying to bite her nails, or the straw with the pretty pink umbrella. Sabrina, having had the experience of writing a book straight from her heart in the most raw real way anyone could ever write, wanted nothing to do with "The Friend" or anything, for that matter, that wasn't real. Nope. The days of fake, almost real, has so much potential to be real, were OVER. Swear on *GirlPower*.

And as much as Fashionista begged Sabrina to "suck it up" and hang out with the "Guys" for the night, Sabrina had no interest. All she really wanted to do was crawl into her comfy cozy bed and sleep peacefully with the security of truth and love blanketing her from the cold chill of counterfeit people who were hell bent on proving how "real" they were.

R and R

The next few months consisted of endless editing and marketing meetings to launch *GirlPower*. The local TV stations had picked up on what Sabrina was doing in her practice with women of all ages and the transformation that was taking place in her little office as the power of love and self acceptance took root to change lives from the inside out. She was being interviewed for segments weekly on top of managing her full-time practice and working with "The Publisher" to get *GirlPower* up and running. And Sabrina, much as this was a dream come true, was weary.

Deep dark winter had arrived with a chill that was unbearable, and Sabrina desperately needed a break to unwind and reconnect with her loved ones. Remember the importance of taking time to connect with the people, places and things you love? Sabrina was losing that connection and knew she needed to make the time now, or darkness and cold would begin to take over.

Kat was feeling weary too, the stress of working full time, managing a marriage and motherhood, mixed with the cold gray days had taken their toll on her energy level and zest for life. She began to feel like a robot, going through the motions of managing a family and a successful career as a genius chemist, and slowly she begin to feel like she was losing herself in the midst of day-to-day responsibilities.

Fashionista, who always had boundless energy, was exhausted herself. She was trying to muster up the courage to walk away from a relationship with a man who was so clearly not for her. Like, pretty much didn't appreciate her unique talent for design and free spirit attitude by which she conducted her life. Rather, he was consistently bored by her creative flare and seemed annoyed by all of her "projects." Sabrina and Kat had tried to beat the *GirlPower* motto into Fasionista's true, genuine full of love, heart, but despite the obvious, Fashionista just couldn't seem to walk away. The fear of approaching 30, launching her design career, and the possibility of being single were just too much for Fashionista to handle all at once.

So, with that, the three weary wino's of Eastwick planned a tropical island getaway for some fun and sun. Every girl knows the best way to rejuvenate and unwind is to head for the sun with your best girl pals.

As they relaxed on the beach flipping through *People* and *US* sipping delicious pretty pink umbrella drinks, Sabrina could not help but think that despite the different places each one of them was in their lives, they were bonded to one another by the unspoken bonds of sisterhood that women share despite the differences in circumstances.

Sabrina had the career of her dreams, and for the first time in her life, had experienced love, only to have to let it go. While she knew her love life would eventually work out, she would be lying if she said doubt did not come knocking on her door to scream, "That's it! You will be alone FOREVER and you will never fall in love again EVER." Some days, she was able to look through the peep hole and not answer, but other days it seemed Doubt had a key and no matter how hard she tried not to engage, it was there just waiting for a vulnerable moment.

Fashionista was in the beginning of launching her design career filled with uncertainty about which road to take, while at the same time, full of fear that she would never have the love she wanted and deserved. And while she knew she should walk away from a relationship that only stifled her, she couldn't let go fully for fear there was nothing better for her in love.

Kat, on the other hand, had found her True Love, married him, had a gorgeous baby girl, and successful career as a genius chemist, who was sought after by Fortune 500 companies. Yet, despite having it all, Kat would sometimes find herself missing the days when she only had to take care of herself and the only responsibility was to plan what to wear for the night of fun with her gal pals.

Sabrina realized, it really doesn't matter where you are on the path, because doubt and uncertainty will always be waiting in the wings. Waiting for a moment when the chill of winter has set in, and life becomes mundane due to the business of responsibility, and that's right when doubt will it swoop in like a vulture, waiting to prey on the vulnerable and weary.

It's just at this moment when no matter what the circumstances are, you have to make time to replenish and surround yourself with warmth and love. These are the key ingredients to keep that doubt from having full on access to your faith and hope.

That's just what the three amigos did. Tropical getaway STAT. Days filled with coconut smelling suntan lotion and evenings of delicious dinners and cocktails, and of course, eye candy for dessert. But truly, none of them were interested in doing nothing more than looking. No way, this was about *GIRLPOWER*: celebrity gossip, a great tan and RESTORATION. Sun and fun rock, pass it on...

After having the best week ever of nonstop laughter and deep soulful talks about Brangelina's now borderline weird obsession to reproduce, Sabrina, Kat and Fashionista returned to the cold with color in their cheeks and faith in their hearts having come to the conclusion, with the help of margaritas and God, that they were each where they were supposed to be on the path, with love, without love, with career, without career, and that was simply, ENOUGH (see *GirlPower* mission statement...and PASS ON)!

THE SWEEDIE

As the three amigo's returned from their much needed R & R, Sabrina was gearing up for multiple meetings in The City with her publishing firm. As a novice, The Firm was concerned Sabrina would be overwhelmed with all of the meetings and decisions she would have to make in going forward with *GirlPower.* They decided to have her work with a publicity agent to introduce Sabrina into the publishing world.

Sven Svennson was his name, publicity was his game. Born in a small farming village in Sweden, he was a self-made man who moved to the United States at sixteen years old in hopes of becoming a model. Never having seen an automobile or tasted a banana, Sven Svennson knocked on every modeling agency door in the country until he became discovered. The Best Ever Modeling Agency signed him on, and overnight, the Swede was world famous. Sven Svennson made it even bigger when he published his rags to riches autobiography. His book became a bestseller and after years of modeling and doing television, radio and magazine interviews, Sven decided to open a publicity firm to help the clueless and naïve of the publicity world...entree Sabrina Davis.

Sabrina was excited to meet him and of course, everyone knew Sven was unattached and a total womanizer. A serial monogamist who dated models and socialites. The rumor was that he was so handsome, girls would get tongue tied and start to blush when he walked into a room. How pathetic, thought Sabrina, no way was she going to fall for his spell. In fact, Sabrina vowed to not fall prey to his charm in any way. She was certain her new found peace and self love would give her the tools to resist any lustful Swedish charm. After all, the Hottie debacle was enough of a wake up call for Sabrina that no matter how charming, you cannot give in to the lustful ways of a handsome man. Unless of course it's been ages since you've been remotely fondled in an indiscreet way, then maybe you can reconsider lust as a cure to potential insanity due to extreme, REPEAT, EXTREME dry spell.

The meeting day is here, and Sabrina is ready to meet Sven Svennson. She wears her favorite black pencil skirt and cream fitted blouse with French cuffs. She thinks this is simple, yet elegant, and that is exactly what she wants to portray. The slutty red leather boots are looked over for the black heels with the shiny red flowers at the top. Perfect, thinks Sabrina, smart and professional, yet feminine and elegant.

Sabrina is escorted into the Best Publishing Firm Ever conference room and greeted immediately by the handsome Swede. Hmmmm, Sabrina thinks, he's early, maybe not so rude after all. She is immediately reminded of the classic Hollywood movie star who oozes quiet confidence and magnetism. You know the type, they go after the leading lady with banter and gusto, and at the end of the movie, they both give in to temptation and share the most glorious romantic kiss, on a staircase, of course.

Okay, snap snap Sabrina, back to Sven Svennson and the business at hand. Right, thinks Sabrina, business. Here are the stats, keeping it to business, of course. The Swede appears to be 40ish, but no one knows for sure because Sven Svennson has NEVER revealed his age. The rumor is he has been 35 for the last 10-15 years, so Sabrina can only speculate that he is 40-50ish. He is over 6 feet tall with the most chiseled, gorgeous cheek bones you have ever seen in your life. Like unbelievably sculpted perfection times infinity. And let us not forget to mention his teeth, perfectly straight white brilliant teeth. He totally has movie star hair, the kind that spreads out perfectly creating a nice little sweep in the front. Blonde, very blonde. Weird, thinks Sabrina, she has never ever in her 34 years of life been drawn to a blonde. They seemed too self obsessed and shallow to the genius, deep, Darling Sabrina Davis Best therapist, now writer EVER.

Okay, back to the Swede…his eyes are warm and sparkly bright blue with flecks of grey. Immediately Sabrina can see kindness in his eyes…his eyes conveyed a joy and sparkle for life, yet within that joy you could see the wisdom that only comes from pain and length of years. Hold Up Girl, Sabrina thinks. This guy is deep and hot!!!

"Helllooooooo," Sven Svennson says in a deep voice with a slight drawl. "I am Sven. It is a pleasure to meet you, Ms. Sabrina Davis."

Sabrina feels warm on the inside. Instead of panicking and freaking out about the tingle in her lower body she feels slightly relieved that she is capable of feeling this feeling, this warmth that reminds you no matter how heartbroken you are, no matter what loss you endure, life continues and we live, mostly for moments like this when our bodies remind us that we are quite capable of experiencing that zing, that shiver, maybe even quiet tingle, that screams, "You are human, you are alive and you will like, love, and feel again!"

Dear God,

Sabrina Davis here. THANK YOU, THANK YOU, THANK YOU that I actually have the capacity to feel something, in this very moment, that is not disgust, or sheer boredom for the opposite sex.

Here's the deal God, he's Swedish, blond and blue eyed, is this a joke? You know how I don't like blondes. Ohhh, and he has good teeth. AND YOU KNOW HOW I LIKE GOOD TEETH, GOD!

Please protect me from lust, and if he is a complete jerk, make it impossible for me to see anything remotely attractive about him. Thanks for listening.

Love, Sabrina.

Okay back to reality. Sven Svennson preps Sabrina from what she can expect from his services as her publicity agent. He speaks with authority, respect and knowledge of this new world Sabrina has been thrust into. As she looks over the contract, Sabrina secretly hopes mind blowing sex and major cuddling with his big huge Swedish biceps are included.

Dear God,
    Sabrina Davis here. Sorry about that shallow, totally lustful thought, but YOU MADE HIM!
Love, Sabrina

Dear Sabrina,
    God here. ALL my children are a work of art.
Love, God

Business meeting over, and Sven looks Sabrina right in the eye, shakes her hand firmly and with a huge classic Hollywood blinding white teeth smile, tells her to be in touch after she looks over the contract. That night, as Sabrina climbs into bed and drifts off to sleep, she finds her thoughts drifting toward Sven Svennson. Within the coziness of her blankets and the peace that the quietness of night brings, she secretly feels her heart hope that Sven Svennson might just be her future Sweedie.

Another One Bites the Dust

Sabrina is awakened by the sound of her phone. She groggily grabs it and looks at the time. Its 5:30 in the morning, and Kat is calling her. Sabrina instinctively knows that something must be up for her to call at this UNGODLY hour. (No offense God.)

Sabrina: What's up?

Kat: I found a condom and a receipt from last weekend to THE HOTEL in THE CITY. I checked his phone. He's sexting a girl. He told me he was on a business trip last weekend. He went with a girl named Trixy. I found pictures of her boobs on his phone. AND they are really nice, perky firm boobs. Appears to never have breast fed which means she is probably a child.

Sabrina can hear Kat take a drag of a cigarette. She wants to ask her bff what the hell she is doing smoking at this hour, but what the hell, if you can't beat em' join em. Sabrina lights a cigarette too and secretly vows to quit after this crisis. Swear on Barbie Shoes.

Sabrina: Oh Kat. Noooooo. Not The Perfect Husband. Ohhhh sweetie.

Kat: I can't believe this. Things have been off since the baby was born, but I never ever thought, not ever, that he would…Oh God Sabrina, What am I going to do????

Sabrina: Kat, you have to talk to him. Be honest…OHHHHH Sweetie I am so sorry. Do you want me to call my friend in New Jersey? Jojo Mance can take care of this…one call and we can make Perfect Husband pay dearly.

Kat: He's awake.

Click.

Sabrina rolls over and hugs her pillow. Queen starts playing in her head…" Deda duh duh duh…Another one bites the dust. Does marriage breed boredom? Are men really capable of committing to one woman?

Dear God,

Sabrina Davis here. What the FUCK! Is this whole marriage deal about if men can't keep it in their pants??? Or women for that matter, sorry to generalize God.

Seriously though, you obviously came up with this concept so why do so many screw it up? Were we really meant to commit to one person????

PLEASE advise. Best friend (besides you of course) in crisis and I need your wisdom here. Get back ASAP! Sorry I said FUCK. I'll work on swearing and smoking tomorrow.

Love, Sabrina

Sabrina was beginning to wonder if anyone remained faithful anymore. The story was the same each time a couple walked into her office. Woman cries.

Man yells then angrily says, "She ignored me, gave me no affection, its all about the kids. I felt lonely. I need love."

Woman cries harder and yells back, "I'm so tired. I try to do it all. You never help me. You neglect me. I resent that I have to take care of the kids and you. I can't be responsible for everyone's happiness."

Entrée Trixy.

Husband: She's fun, she pays attention to me. She thinks I'm a hard worker. You never appreciate me. Trixy loves that I work hard.

Wife: Of course she pays attention to you. She's not managing a household and wiping your kids asses (or managing a career PLUS kids PLUS household). She's not exhausted all the time. She has time to pay attention to you. If you would just help me out more I would have more time to myself.

And that my dears is how it plays out. Woman tired. Man neglected. Trixy saves the day and gives great blow jobs to neglected man. Sabrina had come to realize this: The secret to a successful marriage is this, THERE IS NO SECRET. It takes day to day maintenance and attention. If you brush and floss everyday, you avoid cavities and root canals. If you don't, your teeth fall apart and you have huge dental bills. A marriage is like taking care of your teeth. You have to brush daily with love, affection, respect, and connection. Brush and Floss...Pass it on.

Sabrina Trixy Davis

Kat and Sabrina sip their wine and order seaweed salad and a sashimi appetizer at their favorite Sushi place. Kat's eyes look like she has been pouring shots of pure sodium into them. She's pale and in only a week, appears to have lost ten pounds.

"Wow," says Sabrina, "your jeans look so good on you!"

And Kat laughs. "I dropped ten pounds from my prick of a husband, and we're actually both excited about how good I look in my jeans? We are really sick."

"Yeah," laughs Sabrina, "but your ass looks AMAZING!"

Kat laughs then starts to cry, then laughs again. Snorts, grabs a slug of her wine, cries harder, then goes silent. Sabrina feels her eyes fill with tears and a lump in her chest. She cannot bear to watch her darling pal go through this pain. Sabrina squeezes her hand and waits for Kat to talk.

The day she found the evidence Kat confronted Perfect Husband, and he admitted the affair. Not surprisingly at all, Perfect Husband says Kat ignores him and never wants to have sex with him. Kat says she'd have sex with him all night if he would take out the trash and bring home dinner once in awhile.

"So," Sabrina says, "What are you going to do?"

"I kicked him out. I told him to stay with his parents for a few days. I can't look at him. I told him to find a therapist for us to talk to."

Sabrina nods. "What about Trixy?"

Kat shakes her head in disbelief, "He said he would stop contacting her and that it's just a fling."

Sabrina wonders if she was Hottie's Trixy.

Just a fling…Did Wifey know about Sabrina? Did Wifey feel tired and neglected? Did Hottie go after Sabrina because he was

110

bored and angry at Wifey? Was Sabrina the Trixy that gave Hottie all the hot sex he had been missing with Wifey? What if Wifey just wanted Hottie to help out more and pay attention to her?

It was too much to take in. Sabrina could not bear the thought of being a Trixy. She suddenly lost her appetite. She was sooooo tired of thinking about Hottie. Every time she did, she felt a mix of sadness, anger, confusion, rage and guilt. Guilt that she had willingly dated someone who was separated, or so she thought.

The whole thing made her feel like a huge Trixy, and now, her best friend in the whole world was having to deal with the same scenario. Sabrina secretly felt sorry for Trixy. Did she know Perfect Husband was married with a child? Was she too looking for love and excited at the potential she and Perfect Husband had? Maybe Trixy was just a nice girl who got bamboozled by Perfect Husband's charm and attention. Ugh, thought Sabrina. God Bless and Save the Trixys of the world from lying neglected husbands. PASS IT ON.

George Clooney?

Sabrina has to meet with Sven to look at book cover ideas. She wants *GirlPower* to have a hot pink cover with black bold print. She has in mind exactly how the cover should look and Sven nails it. "WOW, you captured exactly what I had in mind! Sven, this is perfect!"

"My dear, (Sven says in his perfect drawl that screams seduction) I take pride in being so intuitive," he says it with bedroom eyes that make Sabrina feel naked and somewhat vulnerable. She feels herself start to blush and starts to laugh hysterically. She feels her nostrils start to flare, and the snort is T minus two seconds away.

"What?" says Sven.

Sabrina shakes her head and laughs, "Do you always act like your about to film a bedroom scene for the *Young and the Restless?* I mean its weird, you oooze sex out of your pores. Does that crap honestly work on girls?????"

Sven laughs. "Well, I have always thought of myself as a George Clooney type."

"HAAAAA," gasps Sabrina. "REALLY? YOU???? George Clooney????? Try George Hamilton! (Did she mention Sven always had a perfect tan?) Come on George," Sabrina grabs Sven's hand. "Take me for a drink I'm in the mood to celebrate."

"My pleasssssureee," says Sven provocatively.

Sabrina laughs, "I just gagged."

And strangely, Sabrina feels comfortable with Sven. Over the past few weeks of meetings and telephone calls, Sabrina has rid herself of the sexual attraction and is able to work with Sven without constantly thinking about banging him. Their relationship is developing into one of humor and respect. She finds Sven completely vain and strangely sensitive.

Beyond his perfect hair and tan, she could tell Sven was a pretty sensitive guy who probably cried at Hallmark commercials. His vanity was in a twisted way, somewhat adorable. Sabrina had come to appreciate his wisdom and creativity in helping her with the book, and she even found herself enjoying his company. Sven orders two extra extra EXTRA dirty martinis and flashes his Hollywood grin at the bartender. She flashes a grin back and shakes her ass like Shakira as she walks away.

Sven grins at Sabrina and says, "And that my dear, is how it's done…"

"WOW," says Sabrina, "has anyone ever told you that you look just like George Clooney…'s FATHER!" Sven grins from ear to ear and holds his stomach.

"Ohhh, Sabrina Davis, you wicked wicked girl."

Three dirty martinis later, Sven is asking Sabrina why she is so lovely and so single. Sabrina wants to order a bowl of Barbie shoes to nibble on, but decides it's just better to be honest with Sven about her bad choices in love.

She tells him about Hottie, and he just shakes his head. "You my dear girl are naïve, never ever let a guy snow you with charm." Sabrina snorts and gives Sven a punch in the arm.

"This is coming from you? Charm is what you use to bed your collection of girls?????"

"Maybe so," says Sven candidly honest. "BUT, girls like you are too smart to fall for my bullshit. Give yourself more credit than that kid." And with that, Clooney pays the bill and hails a cab for Sabrina.

That night as she drifts into dreamland, Sabrina thinks about Sven. She liked him. He was so honest and real. Or at least seemed to be. He willfully admitted he was a total player and complete fuck up at love. His honesty and self deprecation were refreshing. She liked that she and Sven, ohhhh wait, excuse me, she and George

Clooney, were becoming…friends. Friends? Interesting, thought Sabrina.

POWER THOUGHTS

Every Sunday, Sabrina and Kat had a ritual of going power walking. This meant they put on work out clothes and walked really fast up and down Main Street, power walking in and out of boutiques to check out the new merchandise. Kat was in a surprisingly good mood and was talking in manic mode about her very wise, new therapist, who apparently was also very easy on the eyes. She was going weekly to see him and finding it extremely helpful in communicating with her not so perfect husband, who was still living at his mother's.

As the two BFF's walked briskly catching up on the details of their lives, Kat came out with the question, "WHY, WHY are RELA-TIONSHIPS SOOOO HARD????"

To which Sabrina paused and went into deep, genius therapist mode… She looked Kat deeply in the eyes, shrugged her shoulders and said, "No idea, but what do you think of this dress?"

To which Kat replied by smacking her gum and shaking her head in disgust, "Unless you are going for the lesbian horse trainer look, absolutely NOT."

And with that power talk between them, the girls continued their Sunday afternoon stroll.

Later that night as Sabrina relaxed and took to her journal for some soul searching, she thought about Kat's question. "Why are relationships soooo tough?" And even though Sabrina made it a point to never have a deep thought on the Sabbath, she couldn't help but jot a few notes down on this fascinating topic.

For one, everyone knows relationships take beaucoup effort. But what if, the key to all this relationship stuff starts long before you even meet someone you want to share your emotions, thoughts, toothbrush and bed with?

The one regret Sabrina didn't have is that having had the opportunity to be single for over a hundred years now, (she was certain Willard Scott would acknowledge her centurion status by putting her picture in the Smuker's Jar) she had a pretty good idea of who she was and how she ticked.

EXHIBIT A:

On one such evening long ago, Sabrina was preparing dinner for her and Josh, aka, Lab Geek. She was exhausted, hungry and irritable. Her dear unsuspecting honey thought it would be hilarious to start ribbing Sabrina on her cooking skills. She was experimenting with tofu and beet salad (since he hated meat), and Lab Geek likened her new found passion for tofu to chewing cardboard. On any given evening Sabrina would have had a good chuckle at her own expense, but God help the man who makes fun of an exhausted, hungry woman. When Sabrina told him she really wasn't in the mood to joke around his response was the following, "Maybe you wouldn't be in such a bad mood if you ate normal food instead of this cardboard stuff..." GASP. Immediate spike in blood pressure...

"THERE SHE BLOWS... !!!!" Linda Blair from the Exorcist took over Sabrina's body, and her head spun out of control while her nostrils spewed green venom. She used a voice she hardly recognized. It was a low guttural growl that left her not so sweetie pie like a deer in headlights. The details are foggy due to the adrenaline rush, but Sabrina was pretty sure she used a few choice words and threw a spatula at his head. Before you panic and wonder if she accidentally beheaded the Lab Geek, let me assure you, he actually wins brownie points for his response to her of body experience. Instead of calling her a crazy, hysterical broad on the verge of a breakdown, Sabrina's sweetie ever so cautiously walked over to her, removed the culinary weapon from her hand, gave her a bear hug and said Sabrina put Linda Blair to shame. AWWWW. Sabrina reminded her man of the Exorcist, how adorable.

Here's the moral of the story. If you know yourself, every nook and cranny of how you operate, you can avoid major blow ups by tending to yourself with some TLC and hard core truth. Here's what Sabrina KNEW about herself, Do not, I repeat, DO NOT mess with Sabrina Davis if she is tired, hungry or stressed out.

And while this seems like Relationship 101, way too many people fail to do the work to really figure out what makes them tick. Sabrina wanted to call Kat and tell her this enlightening thought. Maybe, the key to a successful relationship is knowing who you are and what you want, and by the grace of God, Sabrina was getting closer and closer to this every day.

The great thing about getting to know yourself is that this is an evolution that takes place as we open our hearts to learn and grow. The key to this process is patience. And perhaps having patience with ourselves and the paths we choose, is really the most difficult process of all. Why do we put so much pressure on ourselves to figure it out and make it happen? Would if we just stopped, took a breathe, or as Sabrina like to say, SELAH, (which means, pause and ponder this...) and enjoyed the ride? And with that power thought, Sabrina took two melatonin, tried to put herself in a swaddle and slowly drifted into sleep.

S abrina is working insane hours at her practice while bal-
ancing meetings with Sven to launch *GIRLPOWER* into
bestseller heaven. The book is now being printed and Sabrina is
anxiously awaiting the day when she can see her baby birthed to the
world. She checks her email hoping to hear from Sven and sees an
address from a girl she hasn't had much contact with since college.
It's from Goodie Too Shoes who lives in Pleasantville, USA. She
and Sabrina were in the Psych program together and spent every
waking moment studying and running the psych lab experiments
together. It was always fascinating to Sabrina to see the cast of
characters who signed up to be completely analyzed and duped by
choice. As Sabrina would take a certain pleasure in torturing these
poor innocent souls, Goodie Too Shoes would scold her and always
give her the same speech,

"Sabrina, WHAT WOULD JESUS DO??? Please behave
yourself." This always pissed Sabrina off because in her heart, she
believed Jesus had tried to tell these poor suckers all the way to the
psych lab that this was not a good idea, they just didn't listen to the
leading of the Holy Spirit. Poor heathen souls. Goodie and Sabrina
did, however, survive four years of grueling psych lab together and
while vastly different, they managed to stay in touch well past the
college years.

> Dear Sabrina,
>
> I hope you are doing fantastic! (Goodie was al-
> ways a wannabee cheerleader who at any moment
> would clap and yell "We got spirit yes we do, we
> got spirit HOW BOUT YOU?" And Sabrina would
> always want to shout back, "Fuck off Goodie, I was

up all night with the guy from the suite next door and your spirit is ANNOYING." Luckily, Sabrina had matured since then and was much more accepting of people and their ridiculously annoying ways.)

GREAT NEWS! I MET HIM (she always spoke or wrote in caps) HE IS AMAZING! WE ARE GETTING MARRIED AND YOU MUST, NO IF's AND's OR BUT's (was she carrying pom poms when she wrote this?) Sabrina thought. BE A BRIDES-MAID IN MY WEDDING!!!!!!!!!!!!!!!!!!!!!!!!!!!!!!! Love, Goodie and Poopsie (MY NEW HUBBY TO BE! YAYAYAYAYA)

Okay, Sabrina really really wanted to apply all of her *Girl-Power* self acceptance love stuff for Goodie right then and there. BUT she was only human after all! So she lit a cigarette and called Kat to bitch about her unfortunate fate. "Sabrina, you have had such a rough time lately, you really should do it, you'll have a blast!!!"

"Kat, I am 34, did you not get the memo that is practically ancient to be a bridesmaid!!!" FML!

PLATOON

As Sabrina stood at the altar and watched Goodie descend the aisle, she begin to cry. Let be clear here Ladies, these were NOT tears of joy. As she fidgeted in her uncomfortable heels and felt the bobby pins poke at her "up do," Sabrina begin to panic. She was certain she would hyperventilate during Ava Maria and ruin her friend's shining moment.

Here's what happened. Sabrina's mind begin racing with the nagging voice of self-doubt, "What's wrong with you? Why aren't you married? Maybe if you were as committed to finding love as you were to your career, you wouldn't have to do the chicken dance alone…."

That night, as the over enthusiastic DJ announced it was time for all the single gals to line up and catch the bouquet, Sabrina bee-lined it for the bathroom. Let me assure you ladies, you have never seen a woman in spiked dyeables and peach chiffon sprint like this. (Goodie was a traditionalist.)

Just as Sabrina's cold clammy hand hit the door she heard the DJ call her name, "Where's SABRINA??? SABRINA, WHERE ARE YOU GIRL??? THIS COULD BE YOUR LUCKY MO-MENT….GET OUT HERE."

As she tried to dive under a stall, a friend who Sabrina no longer speaks to because of this night, grabbed her hand and pulled Sabrina out onto the dance floor. The TWO girls and Sabrina stood together, a trio bonded together by circumstance, not choice. They stood like women in battle, scarred and bruised as they awaited their fate. Her mouth went dry, and she thought for sure she would hurl her scallops wrapped in bacon everywhere. THANKFULLY, an-other bridesmaid covered in lace and bows caught the bouquet and was inappropriately groped by a groomsman.

Thankfully, that was one battle Sabrina had survived (although she would not have minded the grope).

IT's A GIRL

S ven is laughing so hard he can't breathe. Sabrina, too, is snorting and flaring her nostrils in the most unattractive hideous GAFAAWWW laughter you ever saw. He keeps saying in his smooth velvety voice, "STOP Sabrina, no more, there were ONLY three of you out there, ohhh you poor poor girl."

Sven had called to say they have to have a meeting immediately and he drove up from the City to take Sabrina to dinner. "Sven, I am not joking, this was, in all of my 34 almost 35 years of life, the MOST humiliating moment ever."

"OH GOD," Sven says with a sexy drawl, "I FEEL SOOOO SORRY for you. Well my dear, I have something that may you cheer you up!"

Sabrina wonders if he will give her a pity make out to make up for her bridesmaids gone bad episode. And with that, Sven places a black box with a pink bow onto the table. There is a card attached and for a spilt second Sabrina wonders if Sven is about to propose. Must be the wine, Sabrina thinks.

"What…what is this?"

"Just open it," Sven says with enthusiasm and pride. The card says:

> Dear Sabrina,
>
> It has been my pleasure to work with you. You make me laugh, and while your boobs are not nearly big enough, (thanks Sven) I do my dear, fancy YOU.
> In Lust, Sven George Clooney Hamilton Svennson

Sabrina looks up at Sven and he is grinning ear to ear. Sabrina wants to ask him what the hell fancy means but, she is too excited about the big black box with the pretty pink bow on top.

Sabrina lifts the top from the box and sees her. Her baby girl, a shiny hot pink cover with big black letters *"GIRLPOWER*, by Sabrina Davis." She has never EVER seen a sight so precious in her life. She feels her eyes well up with tears and examines every gorgeous part of this new beautiful creature.

She looks at Sven and he too has tears in his eyes. "Ohhh Sven, she's gorgeous!!!! She looks JUST like..... ME!" Sabrina feels her heart swell. She cannot believe that the day is finally here. Hours of tears, sweat, heartbreak, and labor (with no epidural) and her baby girl is finally here.

> Dear God,
> OMG! Thank you for giving me my baby girl. She is beyond anything I could have ever asked or imagined, YOU ARE THE BEST GOD EVER!!!!
> Love, Sabrina "Best Selling Author" Davis
> Ps- Does fancy mean he likes maybe even loves me?
> Please advise, asap.

A waitress (who Sven decides not to eye bang, thank GOD) brings over a bottle of pink champagne. Sabrina secretly hopes that even Sven realizes it is impolite to show this kind of lewd behavior in front of her new baby. He picks up Sabrina's glass, stands up and walks over to her seat, takes her wrinkly weird hand, picks it up slowly, puts it ever so Sven-like to his lips and says, with complete humility and a sincere heart. "I could not be prouder, she is a work of art, congratulations my dear."

Now Sabrina is sobbing and touching her new baby, every page is perfect, every word is breathtaking. She puts her nose to the cover and feels a slight compulsion to chew the hot pink corner...., but, she realizes Cannibalism is not an option for her child, not unless your plane crashes in the Andes anyway.

As Sven and Sabrina OHHH and AHHHH over her new cre-

ation, Sabrina is floating. "THIS MY DEAR, is time for a CEL-EBRATION…." Sven says with a twinkle in his eye.

With that, Sven, Sabrina and her new perfectly pink baby girl dance the night away in a little hole in the wall place that is dedicated to playing only Frank Sinatra. Perfect, thinks Sabrina, because she is certain God himself has flown her to the moon only to be connected to Sven, her Stranger in the Night, and on no other night has she ever seen a new creation so lovely…just the way she looks tonight.

THE BEST IS YET TO COME

Kat and Fashionista come over the very next morning and are gaga over being a new auntie and Godmother. They both have all sorts of presents for *GIRLPOWER*, which include a new pink Sharpe for Sabrina to do all of her book signings with and a pair of hot pink boots, that they insist, will match her daughter's skin tone and font.

Fashionista pours the wine and asks the question everyone wants to know, "So, what's the latest Kat?"

"Well, we've been going to counseling together. He's really been trying."

"AND…," says Sabrina, wondering if she needs to wipe down her baby with an aloe soothing baby wipe.

"We're dating. He's still at his mother's, but every week we go on a date and are slowly reconnecting. Our therapist says we have to take the pressure off and just learn to reconnect. I don't think he has any idea who I am, or how I've grown. We're taking it very slow…I'm hurt and frazzled beyond belief, but we both screwed up and we need to see if this can work or not. I have a two year old to think of."

Sabrina hugs her baby to her chest knowing exactly how Kat feels, she too would do anything to make sure she stayed connected to her baby daddy (who inconveniently lives in heaven but is faithful at paying child support).

Fashionista stands up and with glee announces, "GIRLS, I dumped his ass and am moving to The City to launch my design collection!!!"

The three amigos cheer in unison and Sabrina can't help but think that for all three of them, as Frank would say, "The Best Is Yet To Come…"

IT WAS A VERY GOOD YEAR

Sabrina's new baby girl took the world by storm. Her book signings were (THANK GOD) lines out the door with hundreds of women all ages, sizes, and colors ready to trade the voice of self doubt for self confidence. Sabrina has to pinch herself to take it all in. In the midst of all the chaos, Sabrina's brother calls to say that he and darling Chloe (aka, Lipstick Nazi) are going to tie the knot in a few months.

Normally, Sabrina would be riddled with anxiety at the thought of sitting through another celebration of love, alone and unattached. Strangely, she feels nothing but peace and genuine, heartfelt congrats for her brother and his new bride. And thankfully, she does not have to be a now 35-year old bridesmaid.

A few weeks later, she and Sven are going over her schedule of book signings for next few months. Sabrina tells him that her brother is getting married and for that week, she cannot have any signings or publicity junkets.

Sven looks at her and gives her his huge bedroom, Young and the VERY Restless, Grin, "And whoooo my dear will be escorting you???"

"Well," says Sabrina with a big grin back, "I wanted to see if George Clooney was available, but I heard he is dating some new chick with size ZZZZ's, guess I have to go alone...."

Sven gives his hearty laugh and grabs Sabrina's very wrinkly hand and says, "It just so happens that George Clooney IS available that weekend, and he LOVES size B's, maybe even on the cusp of C's..." With that, Sabrina has a date for her brother's wedding (and a padded push-up bra).

LUCK BE A LADY

As Sabrina sat in the warm sunshine to witness her brother and his stunning bride exchange vows, she didn't hear the nagging voice of self doubt that stabbed her heart with vulnerability. Rather, as she looked at the blue sky and felt her heart swell with gratitude, she heard the voice of her faithful pal, that had been with her every step of the way....

Dear Sabrina,

God here. You are exactly where you are supposed to BE.

Love, God

And as Sabrina grinned from ear to ear, Sven George Clooney Hamilton Svennson took Sabrina's hand in his and squeezed it. Sabrina was certain that night, she would not have to do the chicken dance alone.

THE BEGINNING

ACKNOWLEDGEMENTS

To my dear friend Meghan Brassel for holding my hand throughout the process of writing this book and teaching me how to use a computer.

Eliza De Rocker for dressing me in style and reading the first few chapters of Barbie Shoes laughing out loud hysterically in applause.

My amazingly creative friends from the Leadership Saratoga Class of 2010: Brett Balzer, Kelly Post Boucher, Garth Elms, Sherri Rose, Michele Southern, Aimee Taylor and Kate Van Buren. Your encouragement in this endeavor has warmed my heart.

My friends at Saratoga Today, Chad Beatty, Chris Bushee, Arthur Gonick and Robin Mitchell for giving me a platform and a voice to write my thoughts to the world.

Gene Yedynak for your laughter, readers, unconditional praise and support in encouraging me to complete what I started. NASTRO-VIA!

Tim Wright, a trusted mentor, respected colleague and ever present Lighthouse.

Debbie Duncan, my FAVORITE teacher who taught me the power of self confidence and to always go after what you want with courage and gusto. I could not have made it through college or graduate school without the tools you gave me in eighth grade reading class. You are a gift and a blessing to me and all of your students!

Deb Heffner for your daily organization, encouragement, kindness and exceptional ability to always keep me in the pink. You are my angel and I am blessed to work with you.

Keely Cameron for bringing Barbie Shoes to life and whose love and support I could not live without.

Open Door Publishers, Inc., Ladean and Joe Adamiszyn, for embracing Barbie Shoes with open arms and giving me this life changing opportunity. Jami LaCasse for your enthusiasm and vision in making Barbie Shoes sparkle!

My amazing family, especially my three siblings, Katharine Lemery Erceg, Elizabeth Lemery Joy and Jay Lemery for giving me a lifetime of writing material. You are the best siblings ever!

My parents, John and Joan Lemery. You have taught me to live life with wisdom, compassion and integrity. Your ever present emotional, spiritual and financial support have given me the tools needed to accomplish my goals and always believe in my dreams. I thank God for choosing you to bring me into the world.

And last but not least, my BFF, the one and only, GOD. Your love and support have been with me always.

Coming soon...

PLEASE PASS THE BABY SHOES

He wanted a boat and I wanted a baby. And here's the thing, I, more than anyone, was the most surprised at this revelation. How did this happen? How did I go from Sabrina Davis content to be in love and in a committed relationship with Sven Svennson to Sabrina Davis, burning desire to be a wife, aka Mrs. Sven Svennson and a mommy? So, I did what every girl does, I pretended I was "fine." I ignored the ache in my chest and focused on how great my life was. Wonderful family, good friends, fulfilling career, solid relationship with someone I adored. I WAS, I SWEAR, FINE.

> Dear God,
>   Why do I feel like I am missing out on something more? What is it I am looking for? Please advise.
> Love, Sabrina

Good old God. I knew, more than anyone, He would help me figure this out. And secretly I hoped that knot in my chest and ache in my heart to merge with Sven would disappear and go away. Somewhere deep inside, I knew that if I let that longing reveal itself, I would have to let go of Sven. It's not that he had ever said he didn't want children, rather, he was great with kids. He could make my five-year old nephew fall into fits of giggles. But I knew that Sven was content in his life. He loved his freedom and he viewed marriage as a ball and chain rather than a loving commitment between two people. He idolized the Charlie Sheen character on *Two and Half Men*, a glorified bachelor who had little interest in commitment or babies, and let's face it, he believed he and George Clooney were separated at birth.

So, rather than put this truth on the table, I avoided the elephant in the room and put on my passive aggressive shield of armor, because after all, EVERYTHING WAS FINE.

I started picking fights with him every chance I got. If he was ten minutes late, I would pout until he scooped me up in a bear hug and tousled my hair, which always disarmed me in a nanosecond. If he picked the restaurant, I complained that I was bored, and we always went there and the service was horrible. If he didn't call me back in a timely manner, I started an all out war about how selfish and emotionally immature he was, to which one day he very maturely replied, "Sabrina, did you ever stop to think that maybe I don't call you back because I don't want to deal with your bitchy attitude?"

Ouch. He caught me. So, instead of telling him my deepest darkest desires to marry him and have his children yesterday, I booked a tropical getaway for his birthday. After all, maybe this urge to merge thing was just a phase that would pass as quickly as crocs or cabbage patch kids. I mean having a baby was a huge life changing event, and I loved my independence and ability to do whatever I wanted to do when I wanted to do it.

Except that lately, whenever I saw a baby commercial or card with tiny baby feet, I would feel tears sting my eyes. (Don't worry, no desire to chew their feet, thank GAWD.)

And then two days before the tropical getaway my brother, Cosgrove, and sister-in-law, Chloe, called to announce that they were expecting a bambino. Instead of feeling overjoyed and beyond thrilled for them, I felt a twinge of sadness, maybe even anger. Something within me knew that if Sven and I were meant to be together for a lifetime, there would be no babies, no call to our family and friends to let them know we had taken the plunge and were bringing a child into the world. Rather, I knew without knowing, our life would be filled with romantic dinners, good wine, travel, elegant clothes, endless Sinatra and great sex. What's not to love about that????

> Dear God,
>> This is so confusing. Please help me.
> Love, Sabrina

> Dear Sabrina,
>> Shhhhhhhhh. Just Be.
> Love, God

So, with those orders from the Big Guy, I decided to BE at one with the ocean and beach while Sven and I lay in the sun and sipped our tropical drinks with the pretty umbrellas. I had put my passive aggressive shield down and decided to be nice to Sven, after all, it was his birthday. And no matter how mad I wanted to be with him the truth was, Sven didn't change, I did.

So, with that I made it a point to be as adoring and affectionate as ever. We spent our days relaxing in the sun and our evenings sipping wine under the moonlight and holding each other close. And one night when we were making love, I became so overwhelmed I started to cry and he kissed the tears off my cheeks and held me close, which only made me cry harder.

In the darkness with just the sound of our breathe and the lullaby of the ocean waves, I said it. "I love you and I want to have a baby with you." There, it was out, and I felt, for the first time in months, relieved.

To which he replied, in Sven Svensson fashion, "Honey, wouldn't you prefer a boat???" Then he did his deep Hollywood game show host laugh and squeezed me closer to him. And I laughed too, because, the truth was, this is Sven, this is the man I love. He is vain, self centered, sarcastic, amazingly warm, sweet, sensitive and pretty damn funny.

I rolled over and took his face in my hands and stared intensely into his blue grey eyes. "Sven, I'm serious, I want to have a baby, I want to make something of our love for one another…I need (pause…) I want…more."

He ran his fingers through my hair and stroked my cheek, which makes my heart melt every time. "Sabrinaaaaaaa……..a baby?"

His face scrunches up showing the fine lines around his eyes. And these are the lines I love. These are the lines and wrinkles that make me feel safe and secure, like he's lived more life than I have and he can somehow lead me in the right direction. Like he knows a secret or key to life that I have yet to unlock. The sixteen years between us has never been an issue, but suddenly I see our age difference clearly and I wonder if these lines between us are thicker and deeper than I know.

"Honey, I'm 50 years old," and then he sort of chuckles, "I would be 70 at our kid's graduation. C'mon baby, be practical!" He takes his hand and runs it through his hair. I love it when he does this because I know that means he is really listening to what I have to say and taking me seriously.

I nestle my head into his chest taking in the clean musky mixed scent of suntan oil and Irish Spring soap, and I start to cry. I feel such a mix of emotions, on one hand I feel like my heart will explode for the love I feel for this man, on the other hand I am sobbing because I sense we are at a crossroads in which I will have to choose, Sven or a baby, but not both. Then there is a great relief that comes with these tears, relief that like all my friends and all the women I love and adore, I, too, have the mommy call. For years I wondered if there was something wrong with me because I had no desire, no call, no ache, to do the baby thing. But now it was here, yelling, maybe even screaming at me to get going.

And now Sven starts to freak out, why, ladies, do men hate it when we cry? It's like they have a control-alt-delete-button in their brain that goes off when the tears start to shed.

"Honey…shhhh," and his words of comfort throw me into the ugly wailing purple face cry. Now my tears and snot are dripping onto his beautifully sculpted strong chest and I think of how much I will miss this chest, and these precious moments between us when we are safe and snuggled up together in bed with silence and peace as our blanket and shield from the cold outside world.

"Ohhh Sabrina, please, don't cry…"

"Please…" I say with my eyes full of tears. "Please just think about it…for me."

"Okay Baby, I'll think about it…"